# zoe
## *Letting Go*

# zoe
## *Letting Go*

## NORA PRICE

razor
bill

An Imprint of Penguin Group (USA) Inc.

razOr
bill

A division of Penguin Young Readers Group
Published by the Penguin Group
Penguin Group (USA) Inc., 345 Hudson Street
New York, New York 10014, U.S.A.

USA / Canada / UK / Ireland / Australia / New Zealand / India / South Africa / China
Penguin Books Ltd, Registered Offices: 80 Strand, London WC2R 0RL, England
For more information about the Penguin Group visit penguin.com

Published simultaneously in Canada

Price, Nora.
Zoe letting go / Nora Price.
p. cm.
Summary: "Zoe goes to a facility to help cure her anorexia as she comes to terms with
the loss of her friend and her own identity"—Provided by publisher.
ISBN 978-1-59514-626-7
[1. Emotional problems—Fiction. 2. Anorexia nervosa—Fiction. 3. Friendship—Fiction.
4. Letters—Fiction. 5. Diaries—Fiction.] I. Title.
PZ7.P93155Zo 2012
[Fic]—dc23

2012012257

ISBN: 978-1-59514-626-7

Printed in the United States of America

1 3 5 7 9 10 8 6 4 2

For A.

Dear Elise,

The woods went on for miles. Hemlock, basswood, cherry, and ash; elms and pines and beeches. Trees crowded against the highway like gawkers at a police barrier, pushing forward for a glimpse of what was to pass. Their arms waved unsteadily in a hot wind as our car moved west on the narrowing highway. I kept my window shut as we drove through this channel of trees, but the sight of them passing—the endless green abstraction—made me ill. When it got so bad that I thought I might throw up, I hunched down in my seat and shut my eyes tight. The trees went on and on until suddenly they stopped, and because my head was bowed and my eyes closed, I couldn't pinpoint when it happened. All I knew when I lifted my eyes was that the car had slowed, and the terrain had changed, and I no longer had a clue where I was.

It was a stupid mistake. I shouldn't have shut my eyes for one second.

Scooped from the woods, as if by a God-sized shovel, stood a wide swath of lawn. The lawn was overlaid by a gravel path wide enough, barely, for one car. I whipped around to see where the gravel path had begun—there must have been a connecting road, after all, for no gravel path merges directly with a highway—but I could see nothing except acres and acres of lawn. I turned to my mother, who steered our car confidently over the path's rough trail, and opened my mouth to ask where we were. But I stopped myself in time.

I knew she wouldn't answer.

School is over. Instead of busted fire hydrants and Cream-sicle wrappers—the sights and sounds of a Brooklyn summer—I currently find myself at the foot of a brick mansion in rural Massachusetts, still wearing pajamas, with a suitcase at my side.

A lot has changed since last winter. My hair is three inches longer, and the second piercing in my right ear has closed up for lack of use. I wear little makeup. I record these changes partly to update you and partly as reminders to myself. Though it occurs to me now that you might be more interested in hearing about the ways in which I *haven't* changed. Those are often more revealing.

I'll give it a try.

My posture is still poor and my penmanship messy. My memory remains pathetic—if you asked me what I did three days ago, for example, I'd have absolutely no idea. None. It's as though my brain is a prehistoric computer with just enough memory to last twenty-four hours, after which point the whole database gets swiped clean. My skin is the same pale shade it was during winter, which is unfortunate given this year's streak of sunny weather. I should have been outside, laying out. I should have put some color into my face. But I guess I've spent a lot of time indoors lately.

The sun's warmth is startling today—when was the last time I stood, unshaded, in full afternoon light? The warmth seeps into my shoes through the flagstone steps. The suitcase at my feet is heavy but poorly packed, and it leans to one side on the gravel surface. Crammed inside are six weeks' worth of socks and shirts and underwear; six weeks' worth of leggings and bras; one toothbrush, one tube of toothpaste, face wash, a bottle of hypoallergenic moisturizer, and no hairbrush. In my rush, I forgot the damn hairbrush.

Is this letter perplexing? I'm sorry. I am doing the best I can under difficult circumstances, and I'm afraid I've gotten far ahead of myself. You must be confused—only after filling a page have I realized that you have no clue where I am or what I'm doing here. To be fair, neither do I. Perhaps I should start at the beginning, at six o'clock this morning, and try to sketch out what I remember.

The sky was dark when I awoke. No morning doves, no thrushes chirping away outside—just the sound of my mother commanding me to get up. "Pack a suitcase," she said. "Pack enough for six weeks."

"What?" I asked. "Why?" I could barely see my mother in the dark. "Where are we going?"

"I'll wait for you in the car," she said, turning away.

"Mom!"

But that was all I got.

Driven by a strange, panic-induced adrenaline, I obeyed her instructions. It felt like some kind of emergency procedure—was Cape Cod being evacuated? Had a disaster occurred in my sleep? When I got into the car, Mom was gripping the steering wheel, her knuckles white. The atmosphere was tense.

"Mom?" I asked again. "Is everything okay?"

She sighed, almost inaudibly. "Put your seatbelt on."

I did, suddenly overcome by a wave of exhaustion. I just wanted to fall back asleep for a few hours. Sleep was on my mind. It had been all I could think of for weeks. I wanted to scrunch down in the seat, lean my head against the door, and forget that the world existed.

It wasn't until the doors locked and the engine revved that I realized sleep would not be a possibility. Because finally, Mom told me where we were going.

Where, but not *why*.

After ten minutes of questions from me—none of

which she answered—my mother turned the car radio to the news station and put on her sunglasses. I sat, stewing, as she listened to traffic reports and weather reports and local headlines. Nothing penetrated my consciousness except for the questions: Why was I being sent here? What could my mother possibly hope to accomplish by stealing me away to a residence like this one? No—not a residence. "Institution" is a better term.

I know what you are asking yourself. And the answer, Elise, is yes.

Yes, you are the reason I am here.

But the answer is a qualified yes. You're not the only reason.

Do you remember the birthday cake I made you last November? You weren't eating cake then; you found the consistency too dry. You were only eating "wet desserts," as you called them. Another one of your funny eating habits. Still, I had to do *something* for your birthday, so I decided to build you a cake out of ice cream sandwiches.

All I had to do was stack a bunch of ice cream sandwiches into the shape of a sheet cake. No baking necessary. Just collect a few dozen premade treats, arrange them attractively in a rectangle, stick a bunch of candles on top, *et voilà*.

Well, not quite.

First, there was a quest to find the correct variety of sandwich. Vanilla, of course, bookended by chocolate wafers. None of that mint-chip nonsense, and absolutely no Neopolitan. Next, I had to get my quarry home on the subway before it melted all over my lap. Back in the cramped apartment kitchen, the cake's assembly presented a true test of my Tetris skills, though I managed to compose a mosaic of the sandwiches before they dissolved into soup. In the end, I spent about ten million dollars on subway fare and an entire weekend sprinting around Brooklyn fetching supplies for the cake. But there was no choice. Your present had to be perfect.

At seven o'clock on November 16, I arrived, tray in hand, at your family's townhouse. The sun was still in bed as I knelt on your stoop, plastic lighter in hand, to ignite each of sixteen candles. Despite their skinniness, the candles emitted a glow that pushed its way bravely into the air's chill. All around me the wind blew, and I wouldn't have been surprised to see a lone Eskimo and his sled trudging past your house on Clinton Street, despite the fact that our coordinates were three thousand miles east of Alaska. It was a bitter morning.

Cake in hand, I struggled up the steps and took hold of the heavy brass knocker. *Tap-tap-tap.* When you appeared at the door, I held out my present, and sixteen candles illuminated your startled expression. Surprise turned to delight, and I knew when you smiled that I'd done a good job. You closed your eyes, held back your hair, and blew out the candles. When you looked up, your eyes sparkled, and suddenly, I understood. You weren't going to eat this cake, either. "Wet desserts" had become "no desserts." If that was what you wanted, I wasn't going to stand in your way. Nobody ever stood in your way.

With a last look at the birthday cake, we exchanged a quick nod to ensure that our thoughts were in the same place. The steps to your house were even icier on the descent, if that's possible, and we barely made it to the sidewalk without slipping. You held the cake delicately, shielding it from the meaner gusts of wind.

"It's beautiful, Zoe," you said.

With a ceremonial flourish, I lifted the lid from the garbage can.

*Thump.*

You dropped the cake into the garbage, where it broke and splattered against the can's dull plastic walls. Beneath the ice cream were bits of orange peel and plastic wrap and wine corks—all the things your family had used and disposed of over the past few days. You replaced the garbage lid, brushed off your hands, and smiled at me through the terrible wind.

"Happy birthday," I said.

Seven months have passed since I marched through the November sleet with that birthday cake in my hands. The date bears no direct relationship to my present, yet my mind keeps returning to that day. To the sixteen candles and ninety M&Ms—brown ones removed—that spelled out your name atop the cake. ELISE. Though I watched those candles sputter out with your breath, they still glitter, in my memory, like a roll of lit firecrackers.

I have learned not to trust my memory on certain matters.

Yours,
Zoe

# [day one]

*My name is Zoe Propp.* I'm sixteen years old and a rising junior. "Rising junior," on second thought, is not a good description for what I am. "Plummeting sophomore" would be more accurate. I dislike green tea, math of all kinds, and brushing my teeth. I like dahlias, navy striped socks, and club soda with a lime.

I love my best friend. Her name is Elise Grady Pope, and she is five-foot-nine with hair so blond it glows in the dark. People think she's Russian or Swedish because average girls from Brooklyn don't look the way she does. But the truth is that she's just like me: a mutt mixed together from too many breeds to count. A little of this, a little of that. Sometimes we'll be waiting at the bus stop and some Toyota with a custom paint job will appear at the curb, bass vibrating so loud you can feel it crawling up your spine.

"Hey girl," the passenger will say. He doesn't need to specify which girl he's talking to because we all know who the target girl is. When Elise doesn't respond—which she never does, at first—he'll try again. "Hey beautiful, what are you? You Polish, or what?" Elise will roll her eyes at me and laugh. Then the guy will say, "You speak English or what?"—as though the only conceivable reason a girl might ignore him is that she doesn't understand what he's saying. Eventually the guy will move on, sometimes yelling, "Stuck-up bitch!" or a similar sentiment in his wake. That's when we really crack up. "Drive-by shootings" is what we call these incidents, and the name would be morbid if it weren't completely accurate.

It's not that we live in a sleazy neighborhood. Our slice of town is more coconut-water Brooklyn than scary Brooklyn, but still, hazards exist. One point two million men occupy our borough alone, and if you're a pretty girl of a certain age, they'll make certain you're aware of it. Part of me inevitably grumbles as I watch yet another car slow down to scope out my friend at the bus stop, not wasting a single glance on the person standing next to her. But then I tell myself, *Zoe! Count your blessings.* I mean, think about it. Would I want every testosterone-addled male on the street imagining me naked? Or worse?

Exactly.

Only the most beautiful girls can afford to forget about their beauty. Both the beauty and the forgetting come naturally to Elise.

I tell you this because I need to remember it myself. By "you" I mean my diary. Or better yet, journal. I loathe the word *diary*—it reminds me of stale cheese and digestive troubles. *Journal* is much better. More dignified. *Diary* is one of my banned words, in fact. Here are some other words I loathe: *menstrual, ointment, spatula, squeegee, breast, pilaf, squat, lozenge, buttocks, lover,* and *stubble.* Oh, and *loin.* I hate *loin.*

But I am digressing. I have told you who I am, thus answering the *who* question, but I have not filled in the *what, where, when,* and *why.* The reason for this is simple. I don't know.

The atmosphere in the car this morning was strained. That might be an understatement—I was a shaken-up soda can of resentments. Jittery and just about ready to pop. Mom calmly manned the vehicle, scanning Route 28 and sipping coffee as though it were any other day—as though we were going out on a bagel run. For twenty minutes I jiggled my left foot and thought of ways to describe how unhappy I was.

"You realize that you're sending me to a labor camp," I said, yanking on the knob that controlled my seat position.

"Zoe."

"Yes. You are. You are taking me against my will to a place where they will make me do things that I don't want to do."

"We're getting you help."

"I don't need help."

"Are we having this discussion again?"

In reply I released the knob on my seat and rammed it all the way back. Mom winced at the noise.

"This is crazy," I muttered, squinting. The sun had risen incrementally as the day progressed, and morning beams were now aimed directly, and painfully, at my eyes. In my stupor I'd forgotten to throw a pair of sunglasses into my bag. Wriggling with irritation, I turned my gaze out the window, where the on-ramp to the Bourne Bridge approached. A sign at the side of the bridge entrance read, *DESPERATE? DEPRESSED? SUICIDAL? CALL 1-800-784-2433.* Jeez. What a cheerful sight. How many people had jumped off before the sign was erected?

"Have some coffee," Mom suggested, interrupting my thoughts. She held out her Starbucks cup.

"There's cream in it," I said.

"You might as well start now."

"Start what? What am I starting?"

Mom sighed and took a sip. Her eyes were maddeningly unsquinty behind dark shades.

"What am I starting?" I repeated. She looked at me wearily, as though I were supposed to know the answer. But I didn't. I had no idea how far we'd traveled from our summer cottage in Cape Cod or how much further we had to travel. I did not know what awaited me at the end of the journey. As for the idea of starting— well, there was nothing for me to start but my summer vacation. Except it was already June, and somehow I was captive to a plan that no one would explain to me. I alternated between feeling like a guinea pig and the victim of a kidnapping scheme. My mother turned the radio up.

The drive was long and monotonous. I scooted back and forth in the car seat, got bored, tried to sleep, and tallied the number of Burger Kings and Dunkin' Donuts by the side of the road. I spotted a Wendy's and wondered why the logo persisted in being so creepy. By mid-morning the car smelled like a road trip—like old mayonnaise and sweat and a banana that somebody left beneath the seat. We drove for six hours, or maybe five. At noon my mother stopped to get a sandwich, which she ate in the car. I wasn't hungry. My eyelids drooped.

I've never understood why car travel is so exhausting. You're sitting there understimulated in every possible way—physically, visually, intellectually—and yet, at the end of the trip, all you want to do is collapse on a comforter and sleep until your eyes are crusted shut.

When I opened my eyes, we'd arrived. Now I've brought you up to the present.

Mom whipped off her sunglasses, got out of the car, and swiveled her head around to take in the view. "Looks like England," she said. "It's gorgeous."

I stared at the building before us. It was a brick mansion, as big as a city library and spreading stealthily across the grounds like a prowling animal. Ten or twelve versions of our cramped Brooklyn apartment could have fit inside the one building easily, though the house's haphazard angles and additions made it impossible to calculate square footage. When Mom popped open her car door, the rush of garden-scented breeze reminded me again of how stale the air inside the car had grown. I wished to deflate like a balloon into my seat, but Mom was having none of it.

"Grab your suitcase, pup."

Aside from its queasy asymmetry, the building's most noticeable feature was its windows, which gaped from floor to ceiling like open mouths at the dentist. Sunlight reflected from the panes, destroying any opportunity to glimpse the interiors. It was a blinding effect, and perhaps intentionally so. To the left of the building stood a vegetable garden, and to the right a broad tangle of roses that was either a flower garden or the unkempt remains of one. The grounds behind me were a map of greenish planes, interrupted, now and then, by miniature groves of oak and beech trees. My legs felt weak and car-fatigued as I pulled my suitcase from the back seat and dragged it toward Mom, who already stood in conversation with a thin, rod-shaped woman who had appeared at the mansion's entrance. The woman was tall, dark-haired, and dressed in red.

"Welcome, Zoe," she called.

*How does she know my name?* I wondered before chastising myself for the unwarranted paranoia. *Get it together, Zoe,* I told myself. It may have been a surprise to me, but this woman, who-ever she was, had clearly prepared for my arrival.

"My name is Angela Birch," the woman said as we approached. "I'm the program director at Twin Birch, and I'd like to introduce you to your new home."

"Temporary home," I corrected. Mom gave me a look.

"How was the drive?" Angela asked. "Not too much traffic, I hope?"

"None," my mother said.

"I'm glad. Shall we begin with a tour?"

My mother followed Angela inside, and I grimly lugged my wheelie suitcase up the twelve stone steps and into the building's main entrance. Inside, it smelled old. Not rotten, but musty—like dust and antique furniture. I paused in the foyer before advancing, looking around to get my bearings. A chandelier supple-mented the sunshine ushered inside by those tall windows I'd noticed earlier, though the hallway itself was nearly empty of furnishings. Angela and my mother were heading into another room, so I rolled my suitcase after them into a closet-sized office. Although a morsel of sunshine found its way into the room by way of a porthole window, the light did little to brighten what seemed an astonishingly cramped room. Instead of being square or rectangle-shaped, the office walls zigged and zagged crookedly, creating acute corners and odd shadows. An aerial view of the space would have been dizzying. As Angela bustled about behind a Japanese-style antique desk, I wondered how she could stand to sit for five minutes in a room that felt as though it were keen on swallowing its occupants alive. Even the ceiling had a menacing stoop. I sat down, pulling my sleeves over my hands.

"The other girls are all in cooking class right now," Angela said, addressing me. "You'll join them as soon as we're done here. Following class, you will have plenty of time to relax, unpack, and explore the facilities."

"Awesome," I said, with a smirk. "I love to explore facilities."

"Cut it out," my mom warned, using the singsong voice she employs when disciplining me in public. As she turned to Angela, her voice was steely and forced again. "It's quite a beautiful location you've got here," she said. Angela smiled gracefully, as though my mother had complimented her on the bacon-wrapped olives at a cocktail party.

"We find it helps for the girls to feel safe and comfortable as they recover."

*Recover from what?* I wondered, pulse quickening. I am healthy and normal. My wrists are not encircled by hospital bracelets, or scars, or any other telltale signs of damage. There is no reason for this. *No reason.*

While Mom and Angela spoke, I glanced at a stack of papers resting on the empty chair opposite Angela's. The pages were printed on thick cardstock and looked like brochures waiting to be folded. When neither woman was looking, I slipped one into my pocket. By focusing on a short-term mission—learning as much about this place as possible—I could calm myself down, I hoped. And remain rational.

Angela retrieved a manila folder from one of her desk drawers and opened it flat on the table, handing Mom a pen. I watched my mother sign the papers necessary to seal my doom, noting that she did so in the same casual way she might use for accepting mail deliveries and signing utility checks. There was a view of the vegetable garden outside Angela's tiny, circular window, and I craned to see what sort of plant matter was being cultivated within it. Peas, tomatoes, and lettuce, all arranged in obsessively geometrical rows. Other green stuff, too.

"Let's see," Angela said, bending over the desk to rifle through the stack of pages. "I think that's it. We're all set for take-off."

My mother looked at me for a long moment, her face as blank as the moon. Then she reached out, still unsmiling, and squeezed my arm. The gesture, though it was meant to be kind, made me bristle. It was the same squeeze she gave me when I was about to have vaccine shots or a tooth pulled—a squeeze meant to prepare me for physical harm. The kernel of anger I'd been toting around was beginning, despite my best efforts, to morph into fear. I felt like a kindergartener on the first day of school, marching into the unknown with nothing more than a backpack for protection. Except this time, I didn't have a backpack. I had a wheelie suitcase.

"I love you," my mother said stiffly, and then—ever the disciplinarian—"Be good."

I kept my lips tightly sealed as we walked toward the door, and it wasn't until I heard tires crunching over gravel that I looked up and around at the hallway in which I stood, once again aware of my predicament. Somehow, it was even worse being here without my mother, despite her responsibility for that very fact. With Mom gone, I knew nothing and nobody at Twin Birch.

Let me emphasize that: Nothing.

Nobody.

My organs turned to jelly. The voice came from behind me.

"Phone," Angela said.

"What?"

"Your phone," she repeated, summoning me back into her office. "And you may take a seat."

I lowered myself into the desk chair opposite hers. It groaned with my weight—was I really that heavy? The thought made me sick.

"There are no phones allowed at Twin Birch," Angela elaborated. "No phones, no texting, no Internet."

She stared expectantly as I dug out my phone and held it, hesitantly, in my palm. How could I surrender my only link to the outside world? I glanced at the screen, but there were no messages. There was no service, either.

"We get poor reception out here, anyway," Angela said, as if reading my mind. "That's the price one pays for privacy."

I gave her the phone.

"You'll get used to the phone rule. It'll help you focus one hundred percent on your recovery."

*My recovery.* It was the second time she'd mentioned it. But what did it mean? From what did I have to recover?

"Okay," I said, my tone neutral and unwavering. Fear was vulnerability—whatever I did, I could not show that I was afraid.

Angela evaluated me coolly from behind her desk before continuing.

"You are the last of six girls to arrive for the summer session. Arrivals are staggered, and no two girls arrive at the same time. For the six-week duration of the session, you'll be expected to comply with the rules of comportment." She paused so that I could signal my acceptance of her statement. When I failed to smile or nod, she simply assumed my response and continued.

"You are prohibited from entering the bedroom of another patient unless given explicit verbal permission."

*Patient?*

"Meals are mandatory, as is adherence to the program. Free time will be allotted according to a schedule, which will be consistent from one day to the next."

I said nothing, but the feeling of panic continued to grow inside of me.

"Aside from today, you won't often see me. I handle the administrative and research aspects of Twin Birch. Your main points of contact will be Alexandra, our in-house psychiatrist, and Devon, our program coordinator."

I barely heard her speech; my mind was still stuck on the

word "patient." I didn't feel like a patient; I felt like an inmate or a victim. "Patient" implied that there was something wrong with me. "Patient" implied that I was sick.

Finished with her briefing, Angela stood and slipped out from behind her desk, plucking the phone from my stunned, open hand along the way.

"We'll keep it safe until you check out," she said with a smile. "Please follow me."

My suitcase squeaked as I pulled it down the hallway behind Angela, keeping my eyes focused on the hem of her suit in order to avoid becoming dizzy. When I chanced a wider survey, I saw that her black hair was gathered into a French twist and secured with a single, glossy chopstick. A pair of pumps rapped against the floor sharply, their assault amplified by the acoustics of the hallway. As we moved away from the periphery of the building, I saw that the house wasn't as bare as it first seemed. Bit by bit, pieces of furniture accumulated: antique mirrors, end tables, settees, statuettes, and ottomans that, by their looks, hadn't supported a pair of feet in decades. Just as I considered complaining about my suitcase, Angela came to a stop before a plain chair and table arranged at the tail end of the hallway.

On top of the table sat a red box, shiny and new-looking among the surrounding relics. But Angela hadn't led me here to show me a box. Next to the collection of items was a door—a closed door.

"Sound-proofed," Angela said, rapping against the door to illustrate her point. "You'll be here every day."

I swallowed hard, determined not to reveal an iota of

bewilderment. Angela scrutinized my face in response, no doubt searching for signs of weakness.

"You're nervous," she said.

I narrowed my eyes.

"That won't last long," she continued, confirming the diagnosis despite my silence. "I'll take you to meet the rest of the girls now. This way, please."

With one hand I grasped the suitcase; the other I jammed tightly into my jacket pocket, where my fingers traced the deckled edges of the paper I'd snatched from Angela's chair. When would I have a moment of privacy to read it? I wanted badly to examine it—*needed* to examine it. The state of semi-paralysis that had enveloped me early in the morning was disintegrating fast. I needed answers soon.

I followed Angela as we headed up a staircase, around a bend, and down a second hallway roughly perpendicular to the one downstairs. As with the ground floor of the building, the rooms upstairs were arranged chaotically, with no apparent logic guiding their placement. Navigating the crooked passages, I realized that I'd need to draw some sort of map in order to keep my compass oriented amid the bamboozling array of corners and half-staircases. After what seemed like a mile inside the maze of the second floor, we arrived at a straight-ahead hallway lined with bedrooms.

"Here we are," Angela said.

I let go of my suitcase handle, and it fell to the ground with a violent thump.

"Well, not quite," Angela amended. "Come this way."

Three bedrooms abutted the corridor, their doors wide open

to show scattered clothes, books, and personal objects. Evidence of inhabitation.

"The bathroom," Angela said, directing my attention through an opposite doorway as we continued. I paused and surveyed the large, white-tiled room. A counter was already clotted with a drugstore's worth of shampoos, conditioners, moisturizers, toners, cleansers, soaps, lotions, contact lens solutions, shaving creams, glosses, serums, sprays, toothpastes, tweezers, and sticks of deodorant. Staring at the bottles and tubes on display, I was reminded unpleasantly of how much effort it takes to be a female. And how much money, too—there must have been three hundred dollars worth of shaving products alone.

My own room was the last of the bunch.

"This is you," Angela said. "If you have any questions about accommodations, I'm sure Caroline or Devon would be glad to help you."

"Caroline?"

"Your roommate."

"Oh," I said uncertainly. *A roommate?* Was I supposed to know this information already? If so, how? I pinched my thumb and forefinger together tightly, which is something I do when my composure is failing me. The presence of minor pain keeps me on my toes.

"Devon," Angela continued, misreading my confusion, "is the coordinator of our program."

I reviewed this information once more. Had I been told about Caroline? I had not. My processing devices were cluttered with new data: the layout of the house, the names of the people, the rules and regulations and schedules. It was a lot for one afternoon.

Especially for a summer afternoon, when my brain wasn't primed for anything.

I wheeled my suitcase into my new room, which was arranged as if for a pair of twins: two beds, two desks, two dressers, all identical. A clean, scrubbed room. The kind of room where you could swipe a finger along any surface, no matter how obscure, and find it free of dust and cobwebs. Nearly everything my eyes swept over was painted or woven of the same color, and the predominant feeling of the room was, therefore, an overwhelming sensation of yellowness. Yellow walls, yellow curtains, yellow lampshade, yellow bedding: Nothing was the same shade of yellow as anything else, but it all belonged to a very specific category of yellowness. The shades were rich and saturate, like shortbread and banana cream pie, or the golden tips of a crisp meringue cookie. I wondered if this was supposed to add up to a subliminal message, and if so, how I would resist it.

One half of the room was a blank slate. Presumably, this was my half. The other half was populated with a dozen items, each organized neatly across the top of Caroline's dresser. I had only a few seconds to eye my roommate's possessions, but a few seconds was long enough for an uneasy feeling to creep up my neck.

"All right?" Angela asked. "Ready to meet the girls?"

I nodded to Angela, signaling that I was ready for whatever came next.

First came the smell. Then came the heat.

I sniffed the air as Angela led me toward the kitchen. Christmas. It smelled like cinnamon, spice, and everything nice. Like wood-burning stoves and ribboned gifts beneath a tree. But it was June, not December, and instead of good cheer, the smell cast a disorienting spell. With each step toward the source, the air grew hotter.

The kitchen was a hybrid of different purposes and shapes, like the rest of the house—a former home kitchen remodeled, with baffling additions and corrections, into an industrial cooking space. Three ovens blasted at 350 degrees each. The room contained three tables, six stools, and six people. Five of the people sat hunched at the stools. The sixth strolled among them, passing out nickel-sized objects. At my entrance the entire group looked up. I pinched my thumb and forefinger together again, praying for the knot of pain to distract me from my nerves.

"This must be Zoe," said the sixth person, strolling over to where I stood. She was solidly built, maybe in her late twenties, with a blond ponytail spouting from the base of her head like a garden hose. Her posture was uncommonly erect, and I could tell she was the kind of person who is genetically engineered to be a camp counselor, soccer coach, or some other middling authority figure. Not a stitch of makeup adorned her confident features, and a light sheen of oil cast a glare from her forehead.

"I'm Devon," she said.

"What's on the menu?" Angela asked.

Devon turned to address the five girls sitting on stools behind her. "Ladies? Want to tell Angela what we whipped up today?"

Five frail girls stared at their hands in silence. I was struck by the hollowness of their features, though perhaps it was an effect of the kitchen's harsh fluorescent lights.

"Tiger milk cookies," Devon filled in. "Smells good, doesn't it, Zoe?"

I nodded automatically—what else could I do? One of the girls at the table glanced up at me with a murderous look. *Traitor*, her expression said, as though by agreeing with Devon I'd already erred. The girl bowed her head back down, letting a wreath of dark curls conceal her face. My stomach heaved. I clearly didn't know the rules here yet. I didn't know who was a friend and who was an enemy. Certainly the gaunt figures in front of me did not look eager to welcome me into their fold.

"We're about to perform the Mindfulness exercise," Devon said, holding up a bag of dried apricots.

Angela nodded. "I'll leave you to it. Have fun, girls." She left without pausing for a reply. I didn't have one, anyway.

I took the only free stool in the room. My table partner was a twiglike creature with blond wisps of hair, a ski-jump nose, and marble-like eyes. Her hands were as dainty as bird claws, save for the thin blue veins visible just beneath the surface. My own hands, by comparison, were as ruddy and robust as a farmer's. I hid them in my lap self-consciously.

Devon placed an object in front of me, then returned to her place at the front of the class.

"Ready?" she addressed the group.

Silence again.

"Put the apricot in the palm of your hand."

I put the apricot in the palm of my hand.

"Imagine you're visiting our planet from outer space," Devon intoned soothingly. "Imagine you dropped in from the moon five minutes ago, and you have never seen anything like this object before."

I looked up sharply. Was this a joke? The girls perched around me stared hypnotized at their pieces of fruit. None would meet my eye.

"Turn it over between your fingers," Devon said. "Explore the texture of the apricot. Let your eyes explore every part of it, as though you've never seen such a thing before."

The reverse side of the apricot looked exactly the same to me: like a piece of scrap rubber. Like something you'd see in the gutter.

"Notice where the light shines on the apricot," Devon said. "Notice where the fruit is dark in shadow."

There was no shadow, only wetness. My palms had grown clammy, and when I tried to pinch my fingers together they slid off each other like peeled grapes.

"Smell the object," Devon said. "While you are doing this, notice any thoughts that come to mind."

The girl next to me held her apricot between two fingers, like an insect. She dangled it one inch from her nose and inhaled. The girl who glared at me was hinged over so that her face was several inches away from the apricot, which lay on the table before her.

I wondered if we were being hypnotized.

"Bring your full awareness to the fruit," Devon continued. "Do you like apricots? What do you like about them? Notice the smell of your apricot."

*Play-Doh*, I thought. It smelled like Play-Doh.

"Gently place the object in your mouth without chewing it."

I looked around. Five girls held the apricot aloft, watching it with the intensity of a chemist mixing formulas. The apricots levitated, but nobody ate. "On three, girls," Devon said, a bit more firmly this time.

What the hell was going on? I raised my hand.

"Yes, Zoe?"

"I'd prefer not to eat this," I said. Five pairs of eyes whipped toward the source of the comment.

"Are you allergic to apricots?" Devon asked.

"No."

Her look was quizzical.

"I don't like apricots," I explained.

"That's fine. But you need to taste it for the purpose of this exercise." Her tone was stringent. Glancing about me in search of understanding, I saw that each of the stares directed at me was an accusation. Had I said the wrong thing again? It wasn't fair—the others had gotten here before me. They knew the rules and they also knew that I *didn't* know the rules. It wasn't fair of them to punish me.

Devon counted up to three. When she got to the final digit, each of the five girls robotically inserted the apricot into her mouth. I put mine down on the table instead. Nobody, I decided, was going to tell me what to do.

"When you feel ready, consciously bite into the apricot," Devon said. "Notice the tastes that it releases."

Five bony jaws sank their teeth into five dried apricots. My apricot remained intact on the table in front of me. I crossed my arms and stared at it. The smell of cookies baking spilled forth, meanwhile, from behind closed oven doors.

One of the girls raised her hand.

"Yes, Brooke?" Devon said.

The girl pointed at me and said, with a mouth full of apricot, "Zoe isn't participating."

My stomach shriveled into a raisin.

"Focus on yourself, Brooke," Devon said. "Everybody with me? Slowly chew the apricot. Notice how it changes consistency. Notice how the tastes change. When you feel ready to swallow, follow the sensations of swallowing down to your stomach."

When the ovens beeped, I glanced up and found Devon eyeing the untouched apricot sitting in front of me. Everyone else, it appeared, had successfully ingested hers. Only one apricot— mine—remained uneaten.

"Good work, girls," Devon said. "You can all test your cookies to see if they're done. Remember to use the mitts; pans are hot."

A scuffle of chairs and murmurs accompanied the other five girls as they rose to fetch their cookie trays. I sat alone, like a child waiting to be punished, as Devon took the empty seat next to me.

"Today is your first day," she said.

"Yes."

"I allowed you to skip the Mindfulness exercise only because I don't like to single girls out right off the bat. The exercises, however, are non-optional. You'll be expected to comply with every step, starting now."

My tablemate returned before I could reply, her tiny arms trembling to support a baking tray laden with glistening brown lumps. "Thanks, Zoe," Devon said, patting my shoulder as she vacated the stool. *Thanks for what?* I wondered. I hadn't agreed to anything. My partner set her tray down on the table, grimacing with the effort.

"Those look perfect." Devon told her. "You're setting a great example for Zoe."

The girl's eyes were glued to the tray, but not even a faint smile curled her lips. The smell of spices and caramelized brown sugar was intoxicating, and I wished I could shut my nostrils the same way I could close my eyes. Devon moved among the stools, hands clasped, evaluating the handiwork of each pair. Dozens of cookies lay steaming on their trays, and the sight seemed to mesmerize the other girls, who ran their fingers over the ridges of the cookies, bent down to smell them, and closed their eyes deeply upon inhaling. Cookies remind most people of home and comfort, but it had been a long time since they reminded me of anything good.

I sat still as Devon handed out fresh copies of the recipe— "For you guys to keep," she said cheerfully. I flattened the recipe page and began to read it, hoping to avoid the stares of the other girls. They were beginning to transfer their interest from the cookies back to me, and despite my best efforts, I felt the stares reddening my cheeks. I felt my back start to buckle under the scrutiny of five girls whose names I did not know and whose histories couldn't possibly be as grisly as their appearances suggested.

One of these girls, it occurred to me, would be my roommate.

\* \* \*

It turned out to be Caroline. Caroline Tilley of Boston, Massachusetts: a girl otherwise known as the hollow-eyed cricket whom I sat next to during cooking class. The empty stool next to her was no coincidence. "You're Zoe," she said to me after we'd folded our recipes and put them away. I couldn't tell whether her remark was a statement or a question, since her tone contained elements of both.

"Yes," I said.

She bit her lip. "You're not what I expected."

"Neither are you," I bluffed. The truth—that I'd been dipped blindly into my situation, and could therefore have no expectations of any kind—was irrelevant. I did not want to reveal my ignorance.

"Hmm," Caroline said, her eyes a pair of bright blue marbles. The conversation ended there.

As we sat waiting for the cookies to cool, I flipped the recipe page over and took notes on the blank side of the paper, hoping that the task would function as armor against the stares that were continuously trained upon me.

*CAROLINE*, I wrote down on the paper, shielding it from her eyes with one hand. *Blond hair. Blue eyes. Cartier watch on left wrist. Nails bitten to the quick.*

I looked around the room to see what other information I could gather. *BROOKE*, I wrote down, cautiously looking in the direction of the brown-haired girl who'd pinpointed me. That was another name I knew. For the others, I simply waited and listened until their names came up—until Devon asked *Jane* to stack the cookie trays, or until *Victoria* and *Haley* were sent to get more paper towels. I wrote down their names and descriptions on the recipe sheet, planning to transfer it in to my journal as soon as I had the opportunity. It would be essential, I knew, to assemble a list of this place's inhabitants and as much biographical information as possible. Only by recording every detail and oddity of what goes on here will I be able to devise the best possible plan of escape. And if nothing else, the contents of my journal will serve as evidence. Nobody believes anything without evidence.

The first installment of my notes follows this entry. I will more add information as it comes.

## Angela Birch
Program director. Not much known.
Age: 50?

## Devon
Program coordinator; instructor of cooking and gardening classes. Strict. Supervises meals and activities.

## Alexandra
Staff therapist.

## Brooke
The girl who called me out for not eating the apricot. Pointy-chinned and shrunken. Thin as a flower petal. Eyes the color of black crayon. Uses dark hair as a crutch: hides behind it, pretends not to hear or see what goes on around her, though I suspect she is observing closely.

Haley

Squeaky voice. Hails from Arizona or Atlanta or some place that begins with *A*—couldn't hear. Red hair, freckles, etc.

Caroline

Hair the texture of straw. Attends St. Agnes Preparatory School for Girls, judging by circumstantial evidence: a St. Agnes Field Hockey T-shirt on the floor of our room and ten picture frames embossed with the St. Agnes crest.

Each picture frame contains a photograph of a baby boy. Identity of baby unknown—Caroline's brother or nephew? Ten seems extreme. To be investigated.

Jane

Ghostly pale. Face the shape of a Mento. Smells of something sour—cat pee? Have not seen any cats on the property.

Victoria

Southern accent, curly hair.

Zoe Propp

Me.

Reviewing my list, I can see only gaps, not answers. There are no men at Twin Birch—why? Why six girls? And why the six of us in particular? The other girls are fearfully skinny and depressed-looking—if it weren't for my unexplained presence,

I'd suppose that Twin Birch was a place for girls who *want* to be this way.

**Tiger Milk Cookies for Silent Observers**
1 cup brown sugar
½ cup vanilla soy protein powder
½ cup wheat germ
1½ cups oats
½ tsp. vanilla
½ tsp. salt
1 tsp. cinnamon
¼ tsp. ground cloves
2 eggs
½ cup canola oil
½ cup chopped dried apricots

Mix all ingredients well. Form into large dollops on a cookie sheet. Bake at 350 degrees for 13–15 minutes. Remove cookies from the sheet before they completely cool; otherwise they will be stuck for eternity.

These cookies are soft and chewy, not crisp. In theory, a person could eat them without producing any noise. If— in theory—a person did not want her whereabouts to be known, for instance, she could eat these without fear of detection.

Later in the day we were given a small amount of time to ourselves. I must have drifted off after I finished transferring the notes from cooking class into my journal because I awoke to a strange yet familiar noise. It seemed to originate ten or twenty inches from my head, and I kept my eyes closed, feigning sleep while I tried to determine what, exactly, I was hearing. It was like the sound of a clogged kitchen sink or an uncoordinated toddler eating soup. But it was neither one of those things.

When I could take it no longer, I opened my eyes to find my roommate Caroline perched bolt upright on the bed next to me, her thumb in her mouth. I stared. *She was sucking her thumb.* A thatch of straw-like yellowish hair and a set of spindly limbs were the only physical characteristics that registered in my mind, aside from the steady in-and-out motion of her thumb. As Caroline noticed that I was awake, her eyes scanned the length of me, moving from face to neck to torso and back up again without revealing the slightest reaction.

"Hi," I said. My tone was not friendly but nor was it unkind.

Caroline jumped, as though my hesitant greeting had broken a trance. She removed her thumb from her mouth and wiped it on the bedspread, where it left a faint trail of saliva.

"What are you doing?" I asked. A simple question.

"Nothing." Her voice was thinner than a napkin and her skin the color of waxed paper; she looked like a girl built from faded scraps of fabric. Her thumb inched its way from the bedspread back into her lap. I could tell she wanted to keep sucking on it.

I decided to try another tack. Perhaps a dash of faux friendliness would help me get some information out of her.

"I like your photos," I said, commenting on the first thing that caught my eye. This was a lie, and as I looked at the photos, I took note, internally, of how creepy they were. Each frame gleamed from a recent polish, and the ornate St. Agnes crest marked the bottom of each.

"Is that your brother?" I asked.

"No."

"A cousin? Or—"

"We're late for dinner," Caroline interrupted, standing abruptly. "It's dinner time."

She walked out of the room, mute as a goldfish. Left without a choice, I followed the sound of her footsteps down the hallway, around a corner, up a demi-staircase, and down a second passage until I arrived at the endpoint of her journey.

*This can't be it,* I thought.

Caroline, who'd arrived a few paces before me, took one of the empty chairs that remained at the center of the room. From the safety of the doorway, I gazed about. Potted palms anchored the periphery of the space, which rippled with the smoke and flicker of candles clustered over two tables. The decor reminded me of the *Titanic,* and I wouldn't have been surprised to find a dotty heiress pouring herself a raspberry cordial with gloved hands, or a robber baron tabulating ill-gotten profits on a cloth napkin. What stood before me was not a dining room at all. It was a time capsule.

And yet, if the ambiance was that of a costume drama, the room's inhabitants were unmistakably of the present. Brooke's thick hair had grown wilder over the course of the afternoon, and it fell in frazzled pieces over the shoulders of a frumpy, stained dress. Jane sat next to her, her straight black hair scraped into a ponytail and her clothes a uniform of anonymity: black cigarette pants, a plain T-shirt, and a pair of low-top Converse shoes. Caroline, who sat with the two of them, wore the baggy pink men's shirt she'd worn all day.

The next table featured Victoria, with honey-colored hair and a white cotton dress with scalloping on the hem. Her shoes, like Jane's, were Converse. Next to her sat Haley, whose red braids mismatched terribly with a long-sleeved red shirt. Except for the zombie-like quality emitted by each one, they looked like any handful of teenage girls plucked from my high school.

I took the chair next to Victoria, sinking into a tuft of pea-green velvet upholstery. At the center of the table stood a pitcher of drooping peach roses and a carafe of ice water wrapped in a cloth napkin. One by one, Victoria and Haley poured themselves glasses of water. The silverware was antique but well-shined, with each piece elaborately engraved. The dining room combined things that I knew very well with things that I'd never seen before, and in this way, it was not unlike a nightmare.

I took a closer look at the two girls who sat at my table. Haley was bony and hollow-eyed, with a dusting of painful-looking acne. She methodically extracted rose petals from the centerpiece of the table and shredded them into tiny pieces. The seat next to me remained empty. I poured myself a second glass of water and sipped, waiting to see if anyone would talk to me. The smell of food hung in the air like an oppressive smog. I methodically spread my napkin in my lap. Time seemed to pass very slowly.

"Girls!" called a voice at one end of the room. Devon.

The six of us turned to face the speaker, whose enthusiasm was the opposite of infectious. On the contrary, it seemed to make everyone in the room more stone-faced than before.

Devon clapped twice. "Everyone hungry?" she asked. It was a rhetorical question, and there was no pause to allow an answer. "Most of you know the drill by now," Devon continued. "Dinner is on the sideboard. Line up, load up your plates, and I'll come around to check up on you. Table one, you go first."

Brooke, Caroline, and Jane stood, gripping empty plates while they floated over to a table at one end of the room. Devon took the empty seat next to me.

"You're going to like tonight's meal," she said, her smile bordered by twin dimples. "Ginger tofu and wild-rice pilaf."

*Christ*, I thought silently.

"What's pilaf?" Haley asked.

"It's a salad made of rice," Devon said. "Lots of whole grains and healthy fats. I think it turned out pretty great, not to toot my own horn."

Hearing this, Haley turned gray. Maybe it was my imagination.

The other table returned with their plates. "Our turn," Devon said, hopping up. Her voice, her motions, her very way of being was at odds with the rest of the group. She was a streak of neon yellow in a sea of charcoal: too loud, too bright, too noxious. Each time she appeared in my sightline, I wanted to look away.

Dishes were arrayed across the sideboard, each in its own silver receptacle: the pilaf, a mound of orange substance, a tray of blanched broccoli, and a loaf of bread coated so thoroughly in seeds and grains that it resembled a porcupine. The ginger tofu was a pile of steaming brown slabs. "I'll serve you tonight," Devon said, taking my plate, "so you get an idea of the right portion size." I watched her place a scoop of pilaf on my plate, a tofu slab, two scoops of orange substance—smashed butternut squash, it turned out—five broccoli florets, and two pieces of bread. Then she handed the plate back to me. I stared at it.

"I'm not hungry," I told her. The food in my hands weighed about the same as a mid-sized toddler.

"Do your best," Devon said. "You're going to have to eat everything on your plate. Seconds and dessert are optional."

I looked at the girl next to me—Victoria—for confirmation of this fact. She gave me a helpless shrug and rolled her eyes. This, I decided, would not do.

"No, thank you," I said, turning back to Devon. I straightened my shoulders and set my plate back down on the side table with a decisive clang, then returned to my table with as much indignation as possible. My act of rebellion, I could tell, sent a ripple through the room.

Privately, my disobedience had plunged me into nauseated unease. A gulp of ice water didn't help to soothe my stomach, so I poured myself a third glass. The three girls at the other table had returned to their seats, where they sat motionlessly in front of their food. Nobody ate.

When Devon returned to my table a moment later, she carried two plates: her own, topped with a mountain of food, and mine, topped with a mountain of equal altitude. She set one of the plates down in front of me as though nothing had happened. The smell of nutmeg wafted up from our table.

"House rules," she said. "Everything on your plate."

Once again I looked at the others, desperately seeking an understanding of some kind. Devon was clearly the enemy, but Victoria, with her small gesture of alliance—the eye roll—seemed like a potential friend. She didn't notice my glance, however, and I watched helplessly as she compressed a piece of bread into the smallest ball possible, squeezing until it was perfectly spherical. She then put the ball into her mouth and swallowed it down with water, like a boa constrictor.

Devon spoke again. "You can take as long as you like," she said. "But you need to eat everything." I watched as she speared a golden raisin from the pilaf, dipped it in squash, and conveyed the massive bite into her mouth. She chewed with relish, her ponytail bobbing.

"It's not negotiable," she added, her mouth full.

"I don't mean to be rude," I said, "but—"

"It has nothing to do with rudeness," Devon interjected. She swallowd her bite. "Rules are rules."

Was I being force-fed?

Gazing around the room, I took stock of the ways in which the other girls were dealing with the menace of dinner. Caroline had not touched her food, but the scene unfolding next to her was a different picture entirely: Brooke, sitting a foot or so to Caroline's right, was shoveling food into her mouth as quickly as possible. On Caroline's other side was pale, bird-like Jane, who bent over her meal like a test-taker shielding answers from a nearby cheater. It dawned on me slowly that of all the sentient beings in the room, Devon was the only one who consumed her food in a way that most humans would recognize as normal. Zesty "mmms" and "yummys" escaped from her lips as she forked fluffy bites of pilaf and slices of tofu into her mouth. She swiped a piece of bread over her plate, catching every drop of olive oil, and closed her eyes with relish as she chewed it up.

With its cargo of miserable diners, the dining room had transformed itself from a decadent stage set to a tomblike enclosure. Candlelight, which is ordinarily so reliable at casting a flattering light, instead deepened Victoria's gaunt cheeks and turned Brooke's under-eye circles from beige to lilac-blue. In the low light, the Oriental rug underfoot looked like an ocean of spilled spaghetti sauce. Indeed, with its shadows and the stillness of its surroundings, the dining room at Twin Birch was imbued with a silence more complete than anything I've ever experienced. It was possible to hear every sniffle, swallow, and bite. Every tearing of bread and clinking of ice. Every moan of discomfort.

*Perhaps this was intentional,* I thought. Perhaps we're supposed to focus on the act of eating, with everything else blocked out. It's impossible to know. I can discern almost nothing about the rules of Twin Birch except that they are detailed and strict, and I would not be surprised to learn that every element of this place has been researched and engineered with a hidden purpose in mind. But what purpose, I had no idea.

Having no choice, I ate my food. But it is hard to eat when you're nearly choking with anger. I'm of the mind that no one should be forced to eat food they dislike—that it violates a basic human principle. It's the worst thing, in my opinion, that you can do to another person.

As I chased each grain of rice around my plate, Devon told me about yet another house rule. Each girl, she told me, was required to stay in the dining room until everyone else has finished her meal. I stared at her when she told me this, unable to imagine the consequences of the injunction. What if one girl refused to eat? What if *I* refused to eat? To prohibit us from leaving the room was unthinkable—it was as though we were a group of hostages roped together. I made a mental note to write the rule down in my journal.

After dinner Devon brought out a couple of containers of Tahitian vanilla ice cream and a basket of fruit from the garden. One girl disemboweled an apricot, but nobody touched the ice cream except for Devon, who conspicuously enjoyed a heaping bowlful. The candles on each table, I noticed, extinguished themselves after exactly one hour. By the time everyone finished eating, none of them remained lit. We sat in the near dark, digesting our unwanted food.

The atmosphere of the room made me think of school, where I first saw girls linger over sparse plates of lettuce dressed in vinegar. Girls clutching cups of hot tea and avoiding the bread basket as though its contents were sprinkled with arsenic. Only girls notice these things, not boys. Boys never see it. After a certain point of thinness, a girl simply disappears from their sightlines.

What followed dinner is almost too gruesome to put in writing. Despite the fact that nobody is reading this, I feel shaky about recording it on paper. If I don't rid myself of the thought, however, I am sure that I will have bad dreams about it, and I do not want bad dreams tonight.

As I brought the last frill of broccoli to my mouth, I became aware of a sound underpinning the scrape of forks and tinkling of ice in the dining room. The sound was low at first, barely perceptible, as though it were emanating from beneath a blanket. When Devon brought out the dessert, she mentioned nothing about the noise, although it was loud enough at that point for everyone to hear it. I swept my eyes from one end of the room to the other, but the noise, it seemed, was directionless. What was it? Where was it coming from? Some inner censor prevented me from asking any questions.

Devon passed around the basket of fruit, which sagged with apricots, plums, and peaches. An overripe scent trailed the basket as I passed it quickly along to Victoria, who took nothing.

The noise grew louder. It was the sound of crabs scuttling along a rocky beach. A dry, hurried sound of tiny claws skittering over tide-washed pebbles.

After the unused dessert plates had been cleared, Devon stood and did her hand-clap again.

"Time to warm up," she announced. Even in the room's obscurity, her skin shone with a reflective layer of oil.

*Warm up?* I thought. She must be kidding. A vision of the five skinny girls (and me) doing calisthenics and light aerobics made me pinch my fingers together. I knew that I, for one, would not be able to move a muscle after ingesting such a great quantity of food. The idea was dangerous. It had to be a joke, I decided—but Devon had not thus far shown herself to be a joker.

We were, at least, allowed to leave the dining room at last. Despite the absence of dinner plates, the smell of food still hung thickly in the air. Devon blew out the two remaining candles, and we got up to follow her, Girl Scout–style, through a pair of French doors that opened into a den abutting the dining area. The candlelight was replaced with art deco lamps that revealed a handful of couches arranged around a hearth, where Devon swiftly began preparations for a fire. She crumpled newspapers, stacked kindling, and positioned a log over the grate, while I watched, baffled by the idea that we would sit before a roaring fire during the middle of summer. Darkness notwithstanding, it was seventy-five degrees out.

The room contained tall cabinets, tall bookshelves, spindly wall mirrors, and a grandfather clock. Victoria was the first person to gravitate toward a cabinet and open it, retrieving from within an armload of white afghan blankets. She passed them out to the other girls, each an eager recipient. *Should I take one?* I wondered. It was awfully hot for a blanket. Why afghans? And why white?

Victoria took the seat nearest to the fire—a fact which I filed away in my mind with a mental asterisk. The seat closest to the fire was the warmest and lightest seat, as well as the only chair outfitted with a matching ottoman. It was the best seat in the room, by far, and Victoria had assumed it confidently, without hesitating to see if anyone else wanted to sit there. Interesting— and decidedly not the action of a person who was insecure about her status in the household. I had a few more things to add to my notes.

Victoria
Southern accent, curly hair. Appears to be an alpha type/dominant

personality. Gravitates toward the position of highest power in any given setting.

Watch out for her.


Anyhow, as the fire crackled and grew, a smell of woodsmoke began to mingle with the faint lavender scent of the blankets. The clock struck nine, and when the chime ceased, I noticed, once more, the strange noise I'd first perceived over pilaf and butternut squash. Crab claws roaming over loose stones. For a second I wondered if I was hallucinating, but when each of the girls had finally gotten her blanket and curled up on a chair or sofa, I saw what I'd failed to perceive for the last hour.

It was not the sound of crabs.

With fire licking the ceiling of the hearth, each girl around me had swaddled herself tightly in an afghan and adopted a hunched position. There were five egg-shaped mounds in total, and from each mound came the sound of chattering teeth.

Despite the heat of summer, each patient at Twin Birch was chilled to the bone.

Caroline sat numbly across from Victoria, thumb hovering near her mouth as she stared into the fire. The collar of her shirt cast knifelike shadows across her collarbones, slicing them into geometric shapes. A pair of thick, grungy rope bracelets encircled her left wrist, and my first anxious thought was that the bracelets performed a concealing function. Was I being paranoid? Maybe so. Chances were I'd find out soon enough.

Next to Caroline were Jane and Brooke, though their positions made it nearly impossible to tell them apart. Each had pulled her legs up tight and was resting her head, face downward, on her knees, revealing only a circle of dark hair to the rest of the group. The only difference was textural: Brooke's hair was fuzzy, and Jane's was slick.

My eye continued clockwise, coming to rest upon the girl who had selected the seat next to me. Haley. I observed her for a moment, taking in the snub nose and brittle, rust-colored hair. Her shins were speckled with bruises.

When she finished laying the fire, Devon came over and sat down next to me.

"Not cold?" she asked.

"No," I said. "It's the middle of June."

A skeptical look crossed her face, as though she suspected me of lying. I saw it, even if it only lasted for a half-second before being replaced with manufactured cheer. I know what she was thinking about me.

"It's common to feel cold," Devon said. "When your body isn't used to digesting that much food."

I stared at her, uncomprehending. I'd eaten large amounts of food before—Thanksgiving, for instance—without needing to wrap myself in thick blankets and roast next to a fire. She was making zero sense.

"When you finally get some nourishment in you," Devon went on, "all of your body's energy goes toward digesting it, and there's nothing left for the rest of your body. Like I said, it's very common, and not something to be afraid of."

I began to understand.

"Zoe," she continued, her face too close to mine. "It's not something to deny, either."

Suddenly, it made sense. As I looked around at the other girls, everything I'd seen so far combined to form a strangely rational conclusion. The cooking classes. The force-fed meals. The frail, stick-like condition of the patients: Twin Birch isn't a hospital, spa, or institution. It is a treatment center for girls who are anorexic.

*But I'm not anorexic*, I wanted to say. *This is a mistake. You've misdiagnosed me.* But the words lost traction in my throat. I could tell that Devon thought I was lying.

The chattering noise grew softer as the fire's blaze radiated throughout the room.

I needed to escape Devon's scrutiny, so I nodded my head at her second offer of a blanket and shrunk down into the sofa, trying to make sense of my predicament. No matter how scientifically I viewed the facts, however, it boiled down to the same mystifying reality: *I'm at a treatment center to cure a disease that I do not have.*

Anyone looking at me can tell you that I exhibit none of the characteristics of an eating disorder. The veins do not bulge from my hands, and my hipbones don't jut. The blanket was stifling, and the food rumbled uncomfortably in my stomach. Each of the girls around me weighed dramatically less. How had I found myself at such a place? Who had thought to put me here? Why was my mother in on it?

As I chewed over these questions, I became aware that the sofa beneath me had dipped slightly with the addition of new weight. Lost in my thoughts, I'd barely noticed Victoria sitting down next to me, relinquishing her position at the fire for a spot at my side. A flush of self-consciousness bloomed in my chest as she leaned closer.

"First dinner is the worst dinner," she whispered, extending a hand. "I'm Victoria."

The loud crackle of the fire masked her whispered words from eavesdroppers, creating a shell of privacy. I shook her hand and introduced myself, cautiously pleased to be making a potential ally.

"How long have you been here?"

"I was the first to arrive. So, four days. All the way from New Orleans."

That explained the Southern accent.

"You're from New York, right?" she asked.

"How'd you know?"

"Please. You might as well have the Yankees logo tattooed on your forehead."

I giggled for the first time in several days. "Mets, actually," I said.

Victoria pointed to the other end of the couch, where Haley sat folded inwards like a collapsible chair. "That's my roommate," Victoria said. "She's solid."

I nodded. "And the others—?"

"Still up for debate," Victoria said, taking in the room with a sweep of her eyes. "Anyway, it's nice to meet you."

"You too," I said, watching as she returned to her original seat. My instincts told me to be careful about interacting with the other girls here, but Victoria's warmth had felt genuine. It was too late to reject it, anyhow. I leaned into the sofa cushion and closed my eyes, dizzy with the effort of thinking. The heavy food must have acted as a sedative because I fell asleep and woke to the grandfather clock chiming the quarter hour and Devon announcing bedtime. As I stood to follow the rest of the girls back to our bedrooms, I saw that someone had tucked a second blanket around my shoulders.

That's when the next step came to me.

# [day two]

*Did someone win the lottery?* Was there a pot of gold in the attic that I didn't know about? A chest of treasure buried beneath the basement floor? I ask because, personally, I've never encountered even a hint of wealth downstairs in the laundry room of our building. Just cockroaches, dust bunnies, and lonesome socks. But someone is paying for me to be at Twin Birch, and last time I checked, my mother's job as a museum curator didn't exactly make it rain on her bank account.

After the panic of last night, I'm starting to calm down and ask practical questions. Sensible, reasonable questions, beginning with this one: How is my mother paying for me to be here?

Let us review the facts of my family's financial situation.

Fact: We live in a rent-controlled apartment the size of a shoebox.

Fact: I've never been allowed to order any drink but water when we go out to restaurants. (Which is rare.)

Fact: I've taken fewer than five taxi cabs in my life.

Fact: When I think of home, I don't think of Broadway shows, sushi dinners, and SoHo strolls. I think of crazy people on the D train, grease-sodden pizza, and sprinting to get on line for discount museum exhibits.

Given these figures, it is somewhat odd to find myself secreted away at an estate lifted directly from a Grimm fairy tale, gilded scrollwork and all. I have to concentrate hard to convince myself that such a place as this exists. I bend down when nobody's looking and run a finger along the parquet floor; I touch the glass of the French doors in the dining room, leaving smudged fingerprints as proof of my being. I am like Hansel and Gretel scattering a trail of bread crumbs behind me, just in case I get lost in this cavernous place.

This is not to say I plan on staying here for long. That would be unthinkable. I am not like the other girls here—not in need of help, not a danger to myself. The only items I've unpacked from my suitcase so far are a pair of leggings (to sleep in last night), a photograph of me and Elise, and my toothbrush. Everything else remains folded and zipped away. If necessary, I can be ready to leave Twin Birch in five minutes.

*Therapy.* The word sounds like the name of a Greek goddess—the patron goddess of whiners, perhaps. There could be a yearly festival in honor of Therapy, if the idea catches on. A date upon which individuals cry, flop around on modular leather sofas, and burn finger-paintings of their parents in effigy.

I read that the high cost of therapy is actually a part of the therapy itself. It works like this: If you pay a lot of money to spend an hour on a stranger's couch, then you will, in theory, place a high value on that hour and make the best possible use out of it. It makes sense, but it also makes me feel dreary about the human condition to think that we're so simple.

Alexandra is not the average therapist. Most shrinks are frumpy—defiantly frumpy. Why? I don't know. Maybe they think that patients will respect the fact that they've disavowed superficial embellishments. The therapist at school is a spherical woman given to pairing animal-print turtlenecks with denim jumpers. I took one look at her on the first day and thought, *This is not someone I should ever take advice from.*

But Alexandra is different. I was following Caroline to breakfast this morning when Angela intercepted my trajectory. She skipped the small talk. "I've set down your first session with Alexandra for eight thirty a.m. today. Do you remember where her office is?"

I did.

"After today," Angela continued, "we'll schedule a regular time slot in the afternoon."

I nodded.

"You haven't eaten breakfast," she said.

I didn't answer.

"We'll make an exception for you to eat during your appointment with Alexandra," Angela decided.

"I'm not hungry."

Angela ignored me. "I'll bring something down in a moment."

She click-clacked away before I could protest, igniting a flare of irritation in my chest. Deep breath. I needed to speak with my mother, since she was the only person who could sort this out and bring me back home where I belonged. She must have been confused when she brought me here. She'd be able to tell Angela and Alexandra that this was all a mistake, and that she'd be coming to pick me up ASAP—yes, that was the solution. I'd be in the car like lightning, slamming the door and discarding the memory of Twin Birch like an old Band-Aid plastered to a skinned knee. Rip it off and throw it out. Now was not the time for hysterics.

As I made my way down the staircase to the office that Angela had pointed out yesterday, I floated on this plan and thought of calm images to set my mood right. Babies cooing, soufflés rising, sea horses floating at the bottom of the sea. If I were going to meet the therapist, I might as well make a good impression. A sane impression. The noises of the dining hall receded as I reached the ground floor, and I began to ponder my strategy. It all depended on what sort of therapist Alexandra was. I've found, over the course of my comparatively short but relatively overstuffed life, that therapists are like teachers: Variations among individuals are great, but certain mannerisms are consistent across the board. For example, all therapists will start a session with a question. A standard entry query. It will be the same every time: "How are you feeling today?" or "How are you?" or "How are things going for you?" The query itself differs among therapists, but it's always the same when you walk in the door. People, like dogs, are comforted by consistency.

Alexandra's door was closed when I got there. How inviting.

I looked at the chair propped outside her door, as well as the adjoining wicker table. The arrangement suggested that I sit down and wait, but I was in no mood to twiddle my fingers. What to do? The red box sitting atop the table gleamed impossibly brightly, as though it had been polished again since the day before. Curious, I tugged on the box's lid to see what was inside—candy? Kleenex? Mints? The lid wouldn't budge. Sealed shut. Only a narrow slit on top of the box provided a window to its contents, but as I bent to peek inside the slit, the door swung open.

"Hello," said Alexandra.

I snapped up like a cartoon rake. "Hi."

"Come on in."

I blinked. This person did not conform to my expectations. Nor did the room behind her.

Stepping inside, I was nearly blinded by the pale office light. I scanned with feeble eyes. Where were the usual signs of a therapist's habitat? The well-traveled Oriental rugs? The house plants? The Navajo wall hangings? This place looked like a cross between an art gallery and a doctor's office: a white cube of a room with minimal furnishings and no smell whatsoever. A sterile zone. A chemist's laboratory. At one end of the space lay a chrome desk and a chest. At the other end, two white leather chairs, a small white leather sofa, and a glass coffee table with nothing on it completed the room. It was as though the entire office had been erased of human sediment. Except for a single box of tissues, it was the emptiest room I'd ever seen. Alexandra herself was dressed head to toe in white. She resembled a Q-tip floating in a giant glass of milk.

"Take a seat wherever you like," she said, folding herself into an Eames chair. I peered at her, taking mental notes for later documentation. Alexandra is a slender woman about the same age as Angela and with the same dark hair, though in Alexandra's case it is chopped into a severe bob that barely skims her chin. The bob contrasted starkly with its snowy backdrop.

I sat down on the sofa. It was surprisingly comfortable. A knock at the door announced Angela, who entered with a covered plate. "Breakfast for Zoe," she said officiously, setting the plate on the coffee table. "They're having whole-grain waffles upstairs, but Devon thought this might be less messy to eat in the office. I'm afraid I didn't have enough hands to bring coffee."

"That's all right," I said, though I wanted coffee.

Angela brushed invisible crumbs from her skirt. "Oatmeal-raisin bread and fruit compote. Hopefully it's still warm."

She left, clicking the door shut as the smell of the bread scented the room. "Smells good," Alexandra commented. A tuft of steam warmed my face as I lifted the napkin to reveal a slab of brown bread, a bowl of purplish fruit, and a spoon. Was I supposed to eat this? Fat chance. The portion was big enough for a lumberjack. I gingerly replaced the napkin and sat back on the sofa.

Alexandra crossed her legs. "It's nice to meet you, Zoe."

"Likewise," I said, not making eye contact. My eyes were distracted by an object that glittered on her hand. A flare of color, sparkling like stained glass.

She noticed my look and held out her left hand, where a bulky cocktail ring bedecked the index finger. "It's a sea turtle," she explained, revolving the ring. "Sometimes it catches the light and creates a glare. Let me know if it gets in your eyes."

I stared at the object. It was costume jewelry, but it looked expensive, somehow. Like one of those antique baubles that rich ladies wear because their real jewels are too valuable to go anywhere except into a locked bank vault. Alexandra's did, it seemed, depict a sea turtle. The ring had four legs, a shell, and a head with diamond-like eyes. Suddenly my mind was fuzzy from the competing sensations of food, glare, whiteness, and sea turtle.

"It's a miraculous animal," Alexandra said. "Do you know that baby sea turtles can swim at birth?"

I did not know that.

"It's true," she said, her diction crisper than rye toast. "Imagine, by comparison, if human babies could walk at birth. Imagine if they could sit up, brush themselves off, stroll right out of the delivery room, and fetch a candy bar for themselves from the hospital vending machine."

I wasn't sure what to say to this, either.

Alexandra's eyes returned to her cocktail ring. "It's wonderful to think about sea turtles swimming at birth," she said, tapping the turtle's shell with a fingernail. "Knowing that such an animal exists makes me intrigued about the world's possibilities."

In the back of my mind, I made another mental note to scout out a similar piece of jewelry on eBay. For Elise's seventeenth birthday, perhaps. Even though I still have four months to find a gift, I know she'd love it. My mind was wandering.

"Can I get you any water? Tea?" Alexandra asked.

"No, thank you," I said. Given that the room contained no glasses, mugs, pitchers, or boxes of tea, I wondered where the drink would come from. My breakfast sat untouched on the coffee table. It smelled as heavy as it looked. I would not be eating it, obviously. The sight of the covered plate alone was making me ill.

But where else could I look? Alexandra sat neutrally, her expression empty but vaguely unnerving. She looked familiar. Had I seen her somewhere—? No, my mind was doing weird things, seeking to draw connections where none existed. I waited for Alexandra to ask an opening question, but she sat motionless and in silence. It occurred to me that the offer of water or tea might have been her opening question, in which case, she was waiting for me to open my mouth.

Well, screw that. Instead I decided to reinspect my oatmeal-raisin bread. I picked it up from the plate, rotated it until I found a corner without too many nuts, sniffed, and put it back down. It was studded with all sorts of suspicious-looking whole grains and looked less like bread than a pile of trail mix formed into a loaf shape. I wiped both hands on the napkin. Now what?

Alexandra spoke. "Do you mind if I ask what you're thinking about?"

I pointed to the slab on my plate. "I was thinking that 'bread' is an awfully liberal description for this thing."

"Ah."

"Why do you ask?" I asked.

"You seemed to go AWOL for a moment. I was wondering where you went."

"Oh. I spaced out."

"What do you think about when you space out?"

I rolled my eyes. "Nothing. I don't know."

"Do you space out often?"

(What was she getting at?)

"Everyone spaces out," I said. "Some people do it more than others. If you're asking whether I zone out during Latin American history class, the answer is yes. If you're asking whether I zone out twenty-four hours a day, the answer is no. Obviously. There's a term for that. The term is 'insanity.'

"Look," I continued. "I'm not going to sit here and try to convince you of anything. Insanity is a zero-sum game—either you're crazy or you're sane, but you can't be both. And I'm not insane."

"I wasn't accusing you of insanity, Zoe. We all create little worlds of our own. We do it on a daily basis."

Okay, so maybe she wasn't calling me crazy.

"Tell me more about when you space out," Alexandra said. "Have you always been able to disconnect?"

"Not always."

"When did it start?"

"I have this one memory," I said. "I was eight years old. My mom has always been strict about letting us watch television, especially when I was little. Cartoons on Saturday was about it. But one night, for whatever reason, she let us eat dinner in front of the TV. Which was a big deal. Major excitement. My brother had control of the remote, which could have been disastrous, except that we instantly agreed on a show to watch. It was about women with extreme plastic surgery. There was one lady who looked exactly like a duck and another who looked as though her face had been assembled from spare celebrity parts. You could actually piece together the individual elements: Angelina Jolie's lips, Halle Berry's nose, Julia Roberts's chin, Jennifer Aniston's hair. The sum total should have been pretty, but it wasn't. It was horrifying.

"Anyhow, at one point I smelled sesame oil and soy sauce in the air. *Mom's making stir-fry again*, I thought. We ate a lot of stir-fry. I could hear the pan sizzling as we finished the plastic surgery show and moved on to a new one about heroic dogs. My stomach grumbled. The entire room smelled like garlic and seared chicken, and I was starving. After forty-five minutes of watching canine reenactments, I got up to go into the kitchen, where I found my mom loading the dishwasher. 'When's dinner?' I asked.

"My mom glanced at me, but continued to rinse out a bowl. 'Stop it,' she said.

"I tried again. 'I'm hungry,' I whined. This time, Mom straightened up and got a furrowed look on her face. 'There aren't any leftovers tonight. Want cereal? Or . . .' She looked vacantly around the kitchen. Then she frowned in a mom-like way—I remember the moment clearly—and came over to where I stood in the doorway. 'Damn, Zoe' she said, grabbing the hem of my shirt and scrubbing at it. 'Sesame oil.'

"I looked down. There was a sesame oil stain on my shirt. But how had it gotten there? Then I realized: I *had* eaten dinner. I'd eaten a plate of stir-fry in front of the TV—probably a big one. Who knows? I could barely remember swallowing it down. I hadn't tasted the food or remembered eating it because I'd been so focused on watching the show. My stomach didn't even remember, even though it was full of broccoli and diced red pepper. That's how out of it I was. Completely gone. On another planet."

I realized how much I'd been talking and clamped my mouth shut.

"What did the experience teach you?" Alexandra asked.

Ugh, what a therapist question.

"Mainly that the average human is crazier than you'd think."

"Do you feel that way?"

I paused. The meaning of her question was unclear. Was she asking whether I felt crazy? Or whether I believed that most other humans are crazy? I hate when adults ask open-ended questions—I hate the phrase "open-ended question," period. Questions should always be specific. That's the whole point of asking them.

Alexandra registered my hesitation. "What we talk about here stays between you and me," she assured me.

"I know."

"The exception would be if I had reason to believe that you were at risk of harming yourself."

"I've been in therapy before. You don't have to read me my rights."

"I see. You know the drill. How about I give you a few specifics, then? While we're on the subject? We can circle back to your memory in a moment."

"Fine," I said. "Go ahead."

"The first rule is simple. If my door is closed, it means I'm with someone. Otherwise, you are welcome to come in and have a chat any time, if there's something you'd like to address outside of our scheduled sessions."

"Got it."

"I'm here from nine a.m. until dinner, but if it's an emergency, you may ask Devon to contact me. I don't live far from here."

This protocol seemed unlikely to become relevant, but I didn't dwell on the matter. Instead I let my attention wander to Alexandra's lipstick, which was the burnt-berry color of raspberry jam. In the white room, her mouth functioned like the signal at a tunnel's end. Why did she wear such conspicuous lipstick? Maybe it encouraged patients to concentrate on what she was saying.

I nodded absently until she finished running through the ground rules of therapy. It was nothing I hadn't heard before in my wide and varied experience with shrinks.

"Any questions?" she asked at the end of her spiel.

"Yes," I said. "Not about the rules, though."

"That's fine. Go ahead."

"Can I be honest?"

"I hope you will be."

*No problemo*, I thought.

"I've been forcibly air-lifted into a house filled with girls who have forgotten how to function like human beings," I said. "My roommate is unbalanced. I slept for two hours last night and have no way of contacting my family."

"That's actually not true," Alexandra interjected.

"What's not true?"

"You can contact your family, Zoe."

I frowned. "That would be news to me, given that I have no phone or Internet access."

"You can write letters."

"Letters," I repeated. "Great. Why stop at letters, though? Why not telegrams? Why not smoke signals?"

Alexandra smiled indulgently at my little tirade.

"How about a pair of soup cans connected by a piece of string?" I suggested. "I hear the reception on those things is great."

"I'm just pointing out that letters are an option," Alexandra said. "Are you cold?"

I looked down at my knees. They were trembling slightly. Had the temperature in the office dropped?

"It's freezing in here," I said. Despite the summer weather outside, my arms were stippled in goose bumps.

"I'm sorry," Alexandra said, getting up from her chair. "I should have offered you something when we started."

She opened a white lacquered chest and plucked a folded afghan from within, where perhaps a dozen identical blankets were folded and stacked in a tower. I blinked at the sight, recalling the chest upstairs from which Victoria had retrieved last night's blankets. How many of these chests were there at Twin Birch? Alexandra handed me the blanket, which I draped over my lap. The material was lighter than a cotton ball.

"Better?" Alexandra asked.

It was better, but I was too guarded to confirm it. I didn't like the fact that she had noticed my chilliness before I had. I get nervous when I can't control other people's perceptions of me. What else had she noticed?

"I try to keep the office comfortable, but the room gets drafty in the morning. Clean blankets are always in the chest, and you're welcome to help yourself any time."

"Thanks," I said, working to keep my voice neutral. Alexandra wore a thin linen tunic and pants, I noticed. But she was evidently unbothered by the frosty air.

"Hot tea helps, too," she added.

I assumed the tea was stashed somewhere in the same chest.

"Picking up from where we left off earlier," Alexandra resumed briskly, "I get the sense that you feel disoriented here."

"No," I replied. "If I felt disoriented, that would mean that the solution would be to orient myself. But this is not an issue of adjusting to my environment. This is an issue of me being in the wrong environment entirely."

"I see."

It was hard to tell if my reply had penetrated her serene, white exterior.

"Perhaps you'd feel better if you spent some time writing a letter today," Alexandra suggested.

"Letters again?" I said, exasperation creeping into my voice. "Are you even listening to me?"

"Very closely," Alexandra said. "Most people, when confused, will either act out or clam up. You've done neither since arriving at Twin Birch."

"Oh?" I said. "Tell me, then. What have I done?"

"You've watched," Alexandra said, leaning in to look closely at me. "You've noticed."

*How would you know?* I thought. *You'd never even seen me until ten minutes ago.* An uncomfortable sense of surveillance caused me to tuck the afghan tighter around my knees. Now that her gaze was focused so intently on me, I wished I could assimilate into the whiteness of the room and disappear.

"You have an eye for the uncommon detail," Alexandra went on. "For the unexpected."

I was silent.

"My ring," she continued. "The red box outside my office door. You noticed both immediately."

"I was curious," I said. "Anyone would be curious about the box."

"Quite the opposite," Alexandra said. "I'm impressed with how inquisitive you are."

"Thanks, I guess, "I muttered. "What's the box for, anyways?"

"The red box is for outgoing mail. I empty it at the end of the day and bring any letters to the post office."

"Oh," I said.

"You sound disappointed."

"I was hoping for a more interesting explanation."

Alexandra stood up and walked to her desk, where she soundlessly opened a drawer. I wondered what she stored inside the all-white drawer in the all-white room—Wite-Out? A bag of marshmallows? Blank sheets of paper? She pulled out a box, closed the drawer, and returned to place the box in front of me.

"I think this will make you feel a lot better," she said. "But you're going to have to trust me."

I wanted badly to know what was in the box.

"The idea may seem strange at first," she continued.

I didn't open the box. To open it would be a form of surrender, and I was not ready to surrender.

But Alexandra was one step ahead of me.

"You can take it with you," she said. "Take it up to your room. Keep it. Use the contents as you see fit."

I nodded, and once again we were left staring at each other in a face-off.

"Has anything else struck you as unusual?" Alexandra finally asked.

Was that a trick question? I answered with appropriate trepidation:

"Plenty," I said.

"Good. Pick one. Pick the strangest thing you've noticed over the past twenty-four hours, and we'll talk about it for the rest of our session."

"The strangest," I repeated. My mind shuffled through my scarecrow-like roommate, the dried apricots, Angela's office, the ghostly figures I'd encountered in the kitchen.

"The most bizarre detail," Alexandra said, prompting me. "The true outlier."

The answer came at once.

"That's easy," I said. "The outlier is me."

Dear Elise,

Day three.

I've always wanted to start a letter that way, like an astronaut beaming in from space. Or a desert-island exile scratching the days onto a coconut palm.

My pen is shaky, and my handwriting shameful. I've been spoiled by years of laptop keyboards. I wonder—how long will it take for human hands to morph into instruments optimized for typing? Not many of us can scribble more than one hundred words without our wrists turning into bendy straws, which is a real shame. I'll have to get my wrists into shape because even after only forty-eight hours at Twin Birch, I have many things to document.

Want to know what I'm remembering right now? The very first party we attended. Or attempted to attend. It was the inaugural weekend of freshman year, which meant that the party would be a landmark event. Attendance was mandatory. Ahmed, the junior who was hosting, made it clear that anyone who planned on participating in the school's social universe had better show up—preferably with alcohol, or, failing that, with attractive friends in tow. Expectations were high, and the stakes were even higher.

By Friday afternoon the air was clotted with anticipation. Our teachers suspected that something was up—the hallways already reeked of cigarettes, perfume, and barely contained anarchy—but they were helpless to stop it. Kids jogged through the hallways and bounced off the walls. Minor rules were broken without a care. It was the first Friday of September—what did anyone expect? For that day and that day only, the inmates ran the asylum.

Ahmed's party was crucial for several reasons. Most importantly, it would set a precedent for the entire semester. Those who hooked up would become couples. Those who acted crazy (in a good way) and those who acted crazy (in a bad way) would solidify their respective reputations. Stories would be generated during that narrow window of time—between eleven p.m. and three a.m. on Friday, September 4—that would carry us through the entire year. Those stories would become currency. Extracurricular currency. If you were at the party, you already had something in common with the cooler upperclassmen. You could tell your own party anecdotes and comment on other people's party anecdotes; you could laugh when someone imitated the guy who passed out on top of a beanbag and had to go to a chiropractor for three months in order to restore his back to its native posture. Or whatever.

If you weren't at the party, you could still laugh at the stories people told. But there would always be the chance that someone would give you a weird look and say, "Wait, were you there?" And if the answer to that question was anything but yes, you could just pack up your dignity and go home.

You and I adhered to a strict pre-party plan all day. We designed a playlist with confidence-enhancing songs. We skipped lunch. We combed our closets for the kind of clothes that would attract older boys without setting off the jealousy sensors of older girls, which is a very delicate equation. At nine p.m. we stopped at Starbucks for two shots of espresso each, treating the bitter liquid like medicine. Drinking espresso on an empty stomach, incidentally, has two effects: One, it makes you jittery. Two, it takes away your appetite.

At eleven p.m., appropriately dressed, coiffed, and caffeinated, we began the twelve-block journey to Ahmed's brownstone. By that time, we figured, the house would be full enough that we could slip in without the awkwardness of ringing the doorbell and making an entrance. It was September, but the temperature hadn't dipped below eighty-five degrees in three weeks. And I was preoccupied, as usual, with the likelihood of my hair frizzing into a clump of wool.

"Crap," you said as we walked. "I'm already sweating through your shirt." You lifted your arms to exhibit a pair of wet splotches underneath. The shirt, a white silk blouse I'd found on sale at Barneys, contrasted starkly with your summer tan. It was the nicest shirt I'd ever bought, and I admit that I felt a twinge of envy at how much better you looked in it than me.

"Not noticeable," I said, focused on smoothing my fly-aways. "Don't worry." What I knew (and you didn't) was that you could have doused the shirt in espresso and no one would have noticed. One of the benefits of being a pretty girl is that you look good in anything, even things that nobody should look good in. Things like turtlenecks and ankle-length dresses and burgundy lipstick.

"But I'm making your shirt smell terrible," you wailed, sniffing. "My armpits smell like curry. Like spicy vindaloo."

"It's New York," I said. "Who doesn't love Indian food?"

This made us both giggle. Another side effect of the espresso.

You were exaggerating, obviously. I smelled not a whiff of curry unfurling from your direction—just the little daubs of vanilla musk we'd applied to our pulse points. Perfume, in general, was against our personal rules, but we made a special exception for the vanilla oil. Perfume was dangerous because it was a clear sign of effort, and in our world, subtlety ruled.

You couldn't go to a party looking like you'd spent more than five minutes putting yourself together. (A mandate also known as the Law of Kate Moss.) Of course, "effortless chic" translated for us non-model civilians into several hours of hair-rumpling and eyeliner-smudging and jeans-cuffing.

When the giggles subsided, you reverted back to an anxious mood. "I hate being at the bottom of the food chain," you said. We were growing closer to Ahmed's. "I don't know anyone there." Having belonged to the small minority of students who had gone to a public elementary school (I'd gotten an academic scholarship, and your grandparents had ponied up the funds when our school district's rating went down), we'd immediately found ourselves excluded from the tight-knit circle of private-school kids who populated our new high school. They all had years of history together—years of shared history and common references. None of them were particularly hungry for outside influences.

"You'll know me," I pointed out. "Plus, there's nothing to worry about because you're the hot one. All you have to do is avoid barfing in someone's lap, and you'll make a good impression. I, on the other hand, have to actively charm people."

"Please."

"It's true," I said. "You can admit it; I won't be offended."

"Stop or I'll barf in your lap."

I cut it out—I always do—but the underlying facts were inarguable. I've never felt competitive about the way you look because it's almost like a matter of historical record: Columbus discovered America in 1492, George Washington never chopped down the cherry tree, Elise is the prettiest girl in the 11201 zip code. Only a moron would contest the matter. If I were awful-looking, it would be tough being your best friend. But I'm okay-looking. If I work at it, I can even be cute.

As we approached Ahmed's address, another sudden change came over you. We both have our moody spells, naturally, but I couldn't put my finger on this one. Maybe the caffeine wore off; maybe the adrenaline stopped circulating. Maybe you remembered something that we were both trying to suppress. Whatever the culprit, we were halfway down Ahmed's block when you stopped dead in your tracks. Further down the block, I could see a thicket of kids arriving with plastic bags of alcohol.

"Can we walk around the block before we go in?" you asked, chewing your bottom lip. "I need to get my bearings."

"Sure," I said, figuring we could each use some encouragement. I checked the time on my phone. Eleven fifteen p.m. "We're ahead of schedule, anyhow."

A distant bass line thumped as we backtracked and hung a right down Hicks Street, which was thankfully empty except for dog-walkers. As we moved away from Ahmed's house, the movement of the party began, perversely, to work its magic on my nervous system. Call it a proximity buzz, but I could almost taste the drink I planned to mix for myself—three ice cubes, splash of seltzer, orange peel, and an icy shock of vodka—traveling down my throat. You and I had discovered the drink that summer when your parents were away, and it made us feel special and cool that we now had a signature drink. My heartbeat sped up to match the bass that pulsed faintly from around the block. A few weeks earlier, I'd been dreading the end of summer. But summer's drowsy tranquility was nothing compared to the excitement of a new school year—the excitement of endless, unexplored possibilities.

As I entertained this reverie, you vanished. Halting, I turned and saw that you'd stopped ten paces behind to sit down on the steps of a dark-windowed townhouse. The orange glow of a street lamp shone down on your slumped figure. I reversed my course and sat down next to you.

"What's going on?" I asked. "Are you okay?"

"Yes," you said. Wisps of white-blond hair tickled across your face. I could hear the slam of taxi doors as more people arrived at Ahmed's. They couldn't see us here. We were safely tucked out of sight.

"It's going to be fun," I said, taking on my customary

role of cheerleader. "You don't smell like an Indian buffet. Not a spoonful. Not even a teaspoonful, which would actually be kind of nice because I'm starving." This didn't get a laugh from you, and I had a sudden and terrible premonition about what would happen that night. A sea change had occurred between point A (my house) and point B (the steps where we sat), and although I had a vague idea of what it was, I didn't want to bring up a subject that we'd agreed to bury.

"Tell me what's wrong," I said.

"I'm trying to forget about it."

I nodded, knowing exactly what you were talking about, and slung an arm around your waist.

"The first week of school—" you started, then stopped. Tears were beginning to sweep fairy trails of mascara down your cheeks. *Oh no*, I thought. Seeing you upset made me upset, too, though at the moment I didn't let myself cry. Unlike you, crying makes me look like a newborn gerbil, which means that I can never, ever cry in front of anyone. I wish I had the ability to look pretty while sobbing like you, but oh well.

"People are monsters," you said.

"They can be," I agreed. Your mood was spiraling downward, and my head was rapidly calculating ways to make you feel better.

"It still catches me by surprise."

"But that's a good thing," I said. "That means you're not cynical."

"Small consolation," you said. "It hurts like—"

"I know." I nuzzled my head against your shoulder, praying that your tears would dry up. My stomach was a pretzel of worry as I sat with my arms around you, wishing—for the first and only time in my life—that I was more maternal and Oprah-shaped, if only to give more effective hugs.

You wiped your cheek, causing a fresh black smear of makeup. "I'm not crazy, right? He'll be there."

"He will," I had to admit, removing the smear with a finger.

"Then I can't go," you said simply.

I couldn't think of anything to say.

"I'm sorry," you said.

"It's okay." Ever since I sat down beside you in the streetlight's circle, my heart had been cringing with anticipation of your meltdown. It wasn't the most generous feeling, but how could I stop it? I'd spent so much time looking forward to tonight. So much time preparing, planning, straightening hair, and plucking eyebrows. Here we sat, less than 400 feet away from the holy grail of freshman year, and you wanted to walk away because one stupid boy had been mean to you earlier in the week. I was torn between utter disappointment and self-pity. But when I saw how unhappy you were, my feelings died down. It wasn't your fault, I knew.

"I can't believe I'm doing this to you," you said, leaning your head against my shoulder.

What could I have done? I did want to go to the party. It was important. But so were you. And in the balance, you were much more important.

I rallied my spirits—there was only one way to deal with this.

"I don't want to go, either," I said as convincingly as I could. "Let's get Diet Cokes and go home. I'll give you a complicated manicure. We'll watch TV and sleep in."

"You're sure?"

It didn't matter, I knew. You'd already made your decision.

"Yeah. If you think about parties objectively," I said, "they're kind of pointless. You go to someone's house and hang out for a while. You drink, see people you sort of know, and cycle through different moods. After a while you go home. Then you wake up with vague memories that are basically the same as other vague memories which you already have. And then you think to yourself, *That was amazing. I can't wait to do that again.*"

You laughed. I was trying to convince myself as much as you.

"Harry won't even be home yet," I went on, struggling to erase any hint of resentment from my voice. "We'll have the place to ourselves."

As we stood up from the stoop, I could hear the whole symphony of arrival sounds from Ahmed's house a block away: cab doors slamming, bottles clinking in brown paper bags, cries of recognition and greeting. We tacitly agreed to take an alternate route home in order to avoid running into anyone we knew.

"Welcome to high school," I said, linking my arm in yours.

"Right," you said. "And I just failed the entrance exam."

"Don't sweat it for a second. There'll be makeup exams."

"You think?"

"Parties are like bodegas," I improvised, as we ducked into a corner deli to buy our Cokes. "There's always one right around the corner."

That was a lie, as we both knew, but a necessary lie. In my book, necessary lies get a free pass on the morality scale. If I'd told you the truth—that avoiding the party would only worsen the catastrophe of the week before—would that have helped matters at all? Would you have felt better?

No.

After all the ups and downs we've been through ever since, the idea of spending this summer with a group of strange girls I don't know—and without *you*—seems absurd. Laughable. As though someone asked me to perform a patently impossible feat: travel through time, turn water into wine, shoot lasers from my eyeballs. In the case of such demands, there is simply no reasonable response.

When our parents sent us to separate camps in fourth grade, we must have exhausted the nation's supply of watermelon-scented stationery and rainbow oily stickers. My supplies are restricted, this time, to plain note cards. But I have much more to tell you. And the stakes are higher now.

Write back.


Love,
Zoe

# [day three]

*I licked the envelope* shut and printed Elise's address on the front, paying careful attention to the clarity of my handwriting. Since I had no return address to include on the envelope, I had to ensure that the sendee was well-designated. The box that Alexandra had given me during our first session contained a wealth of writing supplies—pens, note cards of various sizes, envelopes—but no stamps or postage materials. I figured that Alexandra would add the stamp and the return address later, after I dropped the letter in the red box. Sliding the box back under my bed, I sat cross-legged atop the comforter with Elise's letter. Individually, the envelope and its notepaper seemed to weigh nothing, but when packaged together, the parcel felt heavy in my hands. Substantial. I flipped it over, running my fingers along each edge and waiting for my turn in the bathroom. As I played with the envelope, another sheet of paper popped into my mind.

The memo from Angela's office.

Where was it? I sat bolt upright, half-disbelieving that I'd forgotten about my little acquisition. Rewinding over the past seventy-two hours, I saw myself lift the page from Angela's office on the first day and fold it into my jacket pocket—where, in the subsequent onslaught of adjustments and surprises, I had somehow neglected to revisit it until today. *Christ, Zoe*, I admonished myself, springing up from the bed. I knew my memory was iffy, but I hadn't realized it was *that* iffy. The jacket was stuffed in my suitcase, and I easily located the small rectangle of folded cardstock in the left pocket. One side of the sheet was entirely covered in small type. As I slipped the sheet beneath my pillow, Caroline returned to perform what appeared to be her nightly ritual. I watched her retrieve a soft blue cloth from her top drawer and begin to shine her picture frames one by one. When I returned from the bathroom, she'd finished and gotten into bed, curving herself into a half-moon shape facing the wall. "Good night," I said, to no response. Switching off the lamp, I crawled into bed and waited with ears pricked for Caroline's breathing to grow shallow and steady. Twenty or thirty minutes later, I was certain that she was asleep, though I forced myself to lie mummy-like in bed for an additional five minutes, my hands clasped around the vanilla-hued square beneath my pillow, just to be safe. Once satisfied, I wriggled out of bed and padded outside to the bathroom, taking care not to scrunch the paper loudly or make any noise with my footfall. In a different world, I'd have simply stayed in bed and used the light of my cell phone to read the text-heavy page, but—alas!—my cell phone was locked away in Angela's office. As I shut the bathroom door and flicked on the light switch, I felt my sense of puzzlement harden into determination. What time was it now—eleven? Hard to know. There was no telling how much time I would have in the bathroom before someone got up to pee in the night, so I hoisted myself onto the counter, unfolded the paper, and took a deep breath. Right now, my main priority was to absorb as much raw information as possible. The next day I could comb through the information in my mind and make sense of it while cooking and gardening and otherwise biding time. Smoothing out the pricey-looking card stock, I began at the top.

PURPOSE. *The purpose of Twin Birch is to make a safe and constructive lifestyle accessible to its patients. Located at an estate in rural Massachusetts, the program combines an innovative approach to rehabilitation with elegance and personalized care.*

I reread the paragraph. It said nothing—or did it? My nose wrinkled at the knotty abstractions. I read it once more, but the vague sentences yielded nothing but further vagueness under my eye. If this was any indication, the Twin Birch "purpose" boiled down to a handful of meaningless words glued together with empty adjectives.

I read on.

APPLICATION. *Twin Birch accepts six patients per session. We regret that we cannot accommodate the hundreds of applicants we receive per year. Our current acceptance rate is ~~10~~ 9 percent.*

I stared at the place on the page where the number 10 had been crossed out in blue ink. This was confusing. Given the high quality of the paper, I'd assumed that the paper was a brochure of some kind, but the handwritten edits suggested otherwise. Had I inadvertently grabbed an internal document of some kind? A memo never meant to leave Angela's office?

I read the paragraph again, and this time another detail caught my attention: *9 percent*. "No," I whispered under my breath. *Nine percent?* Nine percent was impossible. Nine percent would make the Twin Birch admissions process not unlike the Harvard admissions process. What's more, I was certain that I'd never filled out an application. (My memory may be shaky, but that's not the sort of chore one forgets.) My eyes were not fully adjusted to the bright bathroom light, and as I scanned the sheet of paper, the sheer density of text began to give me a preemptive squinting headache. For now, the information itself mattered less to me than the origins of the paper. What was its purpose? Without a single image or map, it clearly wasn't a brochure. But neither did it seem like an internal memo, really—why use expensive paper stock for a routine office document? And yet—it was hardly an advertisement for Twin Birch. If anything, it seemed to *discourage* applicants by accentuating the stringency of the acceptance criteria.

There was no way I'd be able to memorize all of it. Instead, I'd have to read as quickly as possible, hide it again, and then write down what I remembered in this notebook the following morning. There was no other option: I couldn't write in the dark, and I couldn't switch on my lamp without waking Caroline. With this plan in mind, I got through three-quarters of the packet before the sound of approaching footsteps jolted me from my research. How long had I been inside the bathroom? *Please don't be Devon*, I prayed, folding the paper back up and shoving it into the waistband of my leggings. I opened the door.

"God!"

Jane jumped back, recoiling from my presence.

"Sorry," I said. "I didn't mean to scare you."

Both of Jane's hands were pressed defensively to her chest, and she seemed on the verge of hyperventilating. *Overreaction, much?* I thought, moving past her into the hallway. "The bathroom's free," I whispered, lifting my chin toward the door. But Jane made no answer, and when I turned to look before heading into my room, she was still frozen solid in the hallway.

# [day four]

*Luckily, last night's* brief interaction with Jane didn't erase the reading I accomplished in the bathroom. I've woken up early today, before breakfast, in order to translate the information I learned as faithfully as possible in this notebook. For organization's sake, I will list the material in a numbered list, with my own questions interspersed throughout.

<u>What I know about Twin Birch</u>

1. Twin Birch is the brainchild of two psychologists, Angela and Alexandra, who founded the program ten years ago in this very house.

2. Originally, fifteen girls were accepted per session [hence all the empty rooms?] but the number was quickly narrowed to six. [Why?] Patients arrive over the course of five days, with arrivals staggered so that each patient can receive a customized initiation.

3. The program consists of four elements: Therapy, Activity, Intake, and Group Downtime.

Therapy means one-on-one sessions with Alexandra.

Activity is any supervised period of physical activity. Our activities are Cooking and Gardening, but past activities, according to the paper, have included Lawn Sports, Origami, Needlework, and Meditation.

Intake is eating.

Group Downtime is the centerpiece of the Twin Birch Experience. It is a concept devised by Angela and Alexandra and refined carefully over the course of two decades. Several articles published in psychological journals and authored by Angela are cited in the paper. Group Downtime itself has four components, the first three of which are set in motion before any of the patients arrive at Twin Birch. Angela and Alexandra select a sample of girls whose disorders and personalities will, according to a private metric, produce favorable results. They choose the girls from the pool of applicants and mail notices offering each girl a spot in one of six annual sessions. Applicants do not get to choose which session they will attend. The enrollment rate approaches 100 percent.

The second step of Group Downtime involves location. It is paramount, according to the paper's explanation, that patients be situated in comfortable, spacious housing stripped bare of technological impediments, like cell phones or laptops.

<u>Third</u>, there must be ample opportunities for patients to spend time in nature.

The <u>fourth</u> step is the simplest. After an elite group of girls has been selected and congregated within the confines of an elegant, leafy location, they are to be left alone.

That's it.

As far as I can tell, the concept of Group Downtime itself is simple; the preparation, microscopically complex. In essence, it is an unsupervised slot of time in which patients are left to their own devices with each other.

This is everything that I am able to remember with clarity. I have a fuzzy recollection of other details, but I'd rather not jeopardize the accuracy of this notebook with guesswork.

As I review my notes, I see that much of the page is devoted to the kinds of clinical nuts-and-bolts that you wouldn't necessarily expect to find in an advertisement or a brochure. I remind myself that the memos were not set out on a wicker table or handed out to patients upon arrival, but stored in Angela's private domain. I wasn't supposed to be reading it.

What does it mean that they don't want us to know this stuff?

My wrist is limper than spaghetti; I need to put down the pen, though I wish I didn't have to. Writing by hand feels like a cleansing habit—like there's something about the physical movement of a pen across paper that hypnotizes me into being honest. I think. E-mail has the opposite effect. The speed of writing an e-mail is an invitation to embellish and omit. It's too easy to type words on a keyboard. Too easy, also, to delete them.

Dear Elise,

I accomplished my getting-ready chores this morning—day number four—like a broken machine. With one hand I rustled around in my makeup bag for the tube of mascara. I brushed it over my eyelashes: left, then right, then left again, then right again. Even a task as meaningless as this—a task that I've conducted approximately 1,095 times in my life—exhausts me at Twin Birch. I stood beneath the cold bathroom light. A zit was emerging on my hairline. A minor event: maybe a 2.3 out of 10 on the zit scale. But still.

If you were here, you'd tell me that it's actually *good* to have a couple of zits on your face because it makes the surrounding skin look even clearer. That's the sort of thing you believe, and your optimism in such things is contagious. "If your skin is too perfect, it just looks like you're on Accutane," you would explain. "Having perfect skin actually makes your skin look *worse*." Usually you're able to win me over with your arguments. If not, you'll simply remind me of your personal motto—"It's not a problem if makeup can solve it"—and unscrew the pot of concealer.

It's easy for you to say these things, of course. Your skin is perfect. Like an actress playing a teenager on TV, your face is unblemished by pimples and stray unibrow hairs. Sometimes when we watch TV together, I secretly compare your beauty with that of the actresses onscreen, and you know what's crazy? You win every time.

That's a rare exception. For all the differences between TV teenagers and real teenagers, the two might as well be a different species. Teenagers on TV win arguments with adults, split desserts in restaurants, don't stain their shirts with toothpaste, and never get their periods. The biggest thing that's missing on TV, though, is this one social phenomenon. It's a single, crucial element of teen existence that goes totally undocumented. Completely ignored. There isn't even a name for it, this thing—it's not a zit, it's not premarital sex, and it's not depression or SAT prep.

It's the reason I live in fear of Group Downtime.

It is the vocabulary equivalent of a black hole. But for me—and for you—it constituted one of the most terrifying daily experiences of high school: the twenty-minute interval between classes.

We'd have "Shakespeare" first period, then a twenty-minute break, then "Colonial Origins," then a twenty-minute break, then "Environmental Chemistry," and so forth. I don't know why our school adopted this schedule, but I'd bet my savings it followed the publication of some research paper that proved a conclusive link between twenty-minute breaks and stellar SAT scores. If that is the case, every copy of that research paper ought to be pulped.

Twenty minutes. It sounds like a snap of the fingers, and it is: Twenty minutes is not long enough to walk the six blocks to get in line for a decent latte, not long enough to complete a meaningful segment of homework, or watch an episode of something on your laptop. However, it's also not a short-enough period of time to pass idly. When you have a small group of friends—or no friends except for one other person—twenty minutes is the precise length of time it takes to become achingly reacquainted with your loneliness.

When I'm at home or wandering around my neighborhood, being alone is relaxing. I don't have to adjust the direction in which I face someone based on the geography of my facial zits. I don't have to worry about my hair. At school, it's the opposite. It is impossible for a person to be more self-conscious than I was during one of those twenty-minute breaks when I couldn't locate you in the halls. On these desperate occasions I did one of three things:

1. Speed-walked through the halls with a purposeful look on my face, as though I were meeting someone to do something.
2. Faked a cell phone conversation. (The most humiliating of social maneuvers?)
3. Hid myself in the bathroom. If nobody else was in there with me, I'd stand at the sink and wash my hands ten times in a row, just to pass time. (My social anxiety is responsible for a forest's worth of wasted paper towels. Trees: I'm sorry.)

Usually I was able to save myself from these charades by locating you. If not, I did whatever possible to avoid standing alone, like a leper, while the rest of the school buzzed and cross-pollinated. I chatted on my cell phone (to a dead line) while browsing walls papered with announcements for plays and basketball games, asking myself: At what point does lingering turn into loitering? And which of those, really, is worse?

Girls are so skilled at finding reasons to dislike other teenage girls. It's always easier to be pretty than it is to be unpretty—trust me—but your looks, I admit, were a problem from the first day of high school. A tall, blond freshman with no concept of—and therefore no adherence to—the school's existing social structure? Forget it. You were toast from the inaugural bell ring on Monday, September 2. And I, your best friend, was collateral damage.

But for the most part, it didn't matter because we had each other. It was during one of those first infernal twenty-minute breaks that we found a little yellow note stuck to your locker. We deciphered the note together in muted awe: It was from a senior named Alex whom we knew by looks alone. He was handsome, nice, and generally excellent at being a seventeen-year-old male, with broad shoulders and a lanky, lopey stride. Written on a torn sheet of binder paper, Alex's note was written in a spidery boyish hand that made my heart flutter. He was asking you out to dinner on Saturday night—the night after Ahmed's party. The note was just a few words long, with his phone number written hastily at the bottom. It looked as though he'd almost forgotten to include it.

"Alex!" you mouthed.

"Dinner!" I whispered.

"Jesus Christ," we said in tandem.

We stared at each other, our eyes googly with disbelief. My head felt as bubbly as a glass of champagne.

In our mind the restaurant date was a relic of the past; most people we knew simply made vague appointments to hook up at a party. But a real date—at a restaurant where waiters and other people would witness the whole thing! What a flattering omen. If this was the kind of thing that could happen on the first day of high school, how could the next four years fail to deliver on such a promise?

"How does he know who I am?" you asked.

"Never underestimate the efficiency of the grapevine

when it comes to transmitting news of hot freshmen," I said. "It's like fiber-optic cable."

People swarmed around us as we examined the note, trying to figure out what the best way to respond would be.

"You're gonna go, right?" I asked.

"I'd be retarded not to."

We pored over the note seeking clues about how to respond. The discovery was so exciting—and the hallway so packed with moving traffic—that I hadn't noticed a girl standing on the stairs nearby, watching the entire episode unfold. Katie Lord was her name, though I didn't find that out until later. All I knew was that a person with curly blond hair and an adultlike briskness to her manner had been observing us as she plucked a pack of Marlboros from her purse, and when she finally swept past on her way out the door, she turned around and addressed you.

"You know that's a joke, right?" A cigarette already dangled from her lips.

Was she talking to us?

"The note," she said, pointing to your hand. "It's a joke. J-O-K-E."

She left.

As soon as she said it, we knew it was true. We'd seen Katie with Alex; it was likely they were even hooking up. Of course the note was a joke. Why would Alex ask a freshman out to dinner? Why would anyone? We'd been idiots to believe it.

A quartet of Katie's friends down the hall had witnessed the prank and were cracking up. Your cheeks flushed so dark it looked physically painful, and I watched, stricken, as you folded the note, walked slowly to a trash can, and threw it away. The bell rang, and we hoisted our bags to go to class, forging an unspoken agreement never to mention the incident again.

It was a watershed moment, though. A milestone. From that moment on, we understood that high school was an arena where acts of cruelty happened as casually as high-fives and sneezes. Alex's note was an accurate indicator of the social landscape. In fact, it was far more accurate than an actual love note would have been.

I don't mean to imply that there weren't nice people and acts of generosity at school. There were those, too. But nothing sticks in the mind like humiliation, and so humiliation remains definitive in a way that kindness does not.

In light of such episodes, twenty minutes can seem an awfully long time. For those on the margins of the social galaxy, twenty minutes offers exactly the right amount of time to feel lost and mortified, like an errant asteroid hurtling through space without a steady course. I suspect that every high school offers its own version of the dreaded twenty-minute break. For some, it is gym class. For others it may be lunch, or that terrible interval of waiting for your parents to pick you up after school while everyone else splits off into couples or groups for post-school socializing.

At Twin Birch, it's Group Downtime. I guess it's not so different here after all.

Maybe we should write a book about similar phenomena when I get home. *Teenage Purgatory: A Medical Encyclopedia of Common High School Ailments.* A definitive work for future generations, with entries on coffee breath avoidance, the perils and pleasures of blogging, how often to wash bras, backpacks versus totes, etc. A summer project to keep us busy.

Twin Birch is supposed to be the inverse of high school, but instead of feeling cozily safe, I'm soaked in a different version of the anxiety that dogged me at home. Here, I'm one of six patients occupying a house with a 1:2 ratio of girls to adults. Even when I'm alone, I have the distinct sense that I am being watched. That my behavior is being tabulated. I've been sleeping poorly, and often I wake up feeling as though my body has been preserved in syrup.

We are officially woken up at seven o'clock by Devon, who strolls up and down the hallway ringing an antique brass bell until everyone is up. The bell is heavy and unpolished, and loud in a way that suggests it may have served, in some past century, as a primitive PA system for a very large house like this one. In its present use, it lends Devon the ability to function as a walking analogue alarm clock. She's very effective in this capacity. Today I was particularly groggy upon waking, and it was only when Caroline poked me in the shoulder that I came to consciousness. Even then, the elements of daylight and activity failed to serve their usual orienting purpose.

Please write back. I miss you.

Love,
Zoe

# [Day Five]

*Of the four Twin Birch* tenets outlined in my purloined paper, Intake is almost as bad as the dreaded Group Downtime. It's hard to have much of an appetite when you're buckling under anxiety, and watching five other girls struggle to eat even a single bite.

Breakfast follows the same pattern as dinner. We eat in the dining room, which looks quite different in daylight than it does in the evening. Devon cooks, and we take turns serving ourselves. If we do not serve ourselves the required amount of food—which nobody does, because the required amount is sickening—Devon ensures that we serve ourselves seconds, and thirds, and sometimes fourths, until we have each eaten to her requirements. How, you might wonder, does a single counselor force six girls to eat everything on their plates? Does she hold a gun to our heads? Does she handcuff us to our chairs?

No, none of the above. It's a wily system they've set up here.

If I weren't the victim of it, I'd consider it a model of simplicity and expedience. The basic rule is this: Nobody is allowed to leave the room until every person has fulfilled her eating requirement. Those who eat slowly, or who refuse to eat at all, must therefore face a wall of peer pressure intense enough to crush a soda can from those who have already finished their meals.

The dining room is swathed in gilded chairs and leafy palms, but it is the least pleasant room in the entire house, and nobody would volunteer to occupy her velvet cushion a second longer than necessary. For those who come to Twin Birch, food is enemy number one, and the dining room reeks of food. The smell of that loathed substance clings to the walls, the carpets, the napkins. With every rustle of curtain, the smells of orange peel and hot bread and basil pesto are released anew. The windows remain shut. I'm not sure if it is physically possible to open them. As long as we languish in the dining room, helplessly pushing grains of risotto and roasted chickpeas around our plates, there is no fresh, clean air for us to breathe. The candles that are refreshed every night burn for an hour before flickering out, and occasionally we end a meal in total darkness.

So we eat. Not willingly, but we eat.

This morning I stood in line with my plate in order to receive a stack of thick, steaming discs topped with honey, almond butter, and fresh cherries. The discs resembled pancakes in shape but not in any other dimension: They were a dark gray color, and instead of hot dough they smelled like crushed walnuts. My tablemates were Haley and Victoria, both of whom I've been sitting with since Victoria introduced herself on my first day.

Haley lifted a pancake with two fingers and dropped it. The disc was so heavy it produced an audible thud. "What . . . the . . . hell?" she groaned.

"Buckwheat pancakes," Victoria explained. "High in protein, low in flavor."

"Close your eyes," I suggested. "It'll taste just like a beignet."

"I oughtta slap you for that," Victoria said, her Southern accent twanging. "In the face. With a pancake."

Haley giggled, causing her red braids to shudder. Victoria remained wry, smiling with a pair of doll-like lips that looked as though somebody drew them on with a fine-tipped pen. If she weren't so frail, she'd be beautiful. Haley is her little sidekick.

"What are these things anyway?" Haley asked, staring at her plate. "What's buckwheat?"

"Have you ever had soba noodles?" I asked. "It's what they use to make soba noodles."

"We don't have those in Phoenix."

"They're kind of nutty," Victoria said. "Not that bad. It's the texture that's a problem." She prodded a pancake with her fork. "Feels like a fake boob."

I poked my stack with a finger, avoiding the slick of almond butter that surrounded it like a moat. "Whoa, yeah," I said. "Firm, yet squishy."

"Victoria's Secret is gonna have a Buckwheat Pancake Bra in six months, bet on it," she said. "These things keep you full forever. You can eat two pancakes and not be hungry until dinner."

"Are they bad for you?" Haley asked.

"No, that's the thing. They're supposed to be healthy."

I ate one cherry, and then another. Neither Victoria nor Haley was eating her food, though each conducted a separate ritual while we talked. Haley counted her cherries (sixteen), cut each one in half (thirty-two), and isolated them on the left side of her plate. Then she scraped all of the almond butter off the pancakes and dammed it on the right side of her plate. Finally, she sliced each pancake into tiny bite-sized pieces, piled them in the center (bookended by almond butter and fruit), and, as a finale, pushed her plate away without transferring a single item to her mouth.

Victoria took a simpler approach. She mashed her food together with a fork, then compressed it into a hockey puck.

At the other table, Caroline was engaged in a staring contest with her food. She wore a sleeveless yellow polo shirt that exacerbated the thinness of her shoulders, which were so angular and sharp-edged that they looked like something out of a Cubist painting. I didn't even know that shoulders had so many bones. There was no padding left. How could she move her arms, I wondered, without making a clicking sound?

Next to Caroline sat Jane, who raked her fork through the almond butter, creating cross-hatch patterns that quickly melted away. To her left, Brooke was engaged in a private discussion with Devon. Unlike the rest of us, Brooke had emptied her plate, though not without creating a mess: Her smock dress was covered in smears of brown and red. Spattered against the green cotton dress, it looked like blood—even when you reminded yourself that it was only nut butter and cherry juice. I leaned as far backward as I could without looking conspicuous, but I wasn't able to hear what Devon and Brooke were saying.

A choking sound filled the air as Haley began crying. Devon appeared at her side, and the two of them engaged in a private conference while Victoria and I looked down at our plates. "I don't want to do it," Haley said, her voice stuttering with sobs. From the other table, Brooke looked over and rolled her eyes with exasperation.

"What's the problem?" she said, addressing Haley. "Do you understand that you're making everyone else wait?"

"I—" Haley blubbered.

"Brooke, please," Devon said.

Brooke folded her arms and sat back, her eyes glued to Haley's shuddering back.

Victoria and I had both managed to shovel down our pancakes, but Victoria hadn't eaten anything else on her plate. "If I eat another pancake, can I *not* eat the almond butter?" she asked Devon, trying to negotiate a deal.

"No."

"If I—"

"Victoria," Devon said, her voice a warning. Haley, meanwhile, had partially recovered from her fit and was lifting a cherry toward her lips. *Come on*, I silently urged, praying that she'd swallow her food. The cherry wavered an inch from her mouth. *Almost there*, I thought. *Just one more inch* ...

Her fork clattered against the plate, splattering cherry pieces all over the tablecloth. *Dammit*, I thought, as Haley began crying again. "She can't help it," Victoria mouthed at me with a shrug. Brooke and Jane, at the next table, shot daggers at Haley, who tried not to notice. Caroline was perched blankly at the edge of her seat, staring into the middle distance as though she'd been immobilized. I sighed and fidgeted until Haley finished, my limbs twitching with impatience.

I'd finished my own breakfast an hour earlier, starting with the cherries and moving on to the almond butter. Following Victoria's example, I took a small, exploratory bite of pancake, willing myself not to gag. *How odd*, I thought, chewing—it tasted nothing like a regular pancake. I took a second bite. If normal pancakes are little more than a blank canvas for butter and syrup, these had a taste of their own. A strong taste, too—like something a miner would have eaten in 1850 before heading out to pan for gold at Sutter's Mill. They tasted old-fashioned.

Somehow, I managed to get through the whole stack. And Victoria was right: By the time I finished, I knew that I wouldn't be hungry again for days.

**Buckwheat Pancakes for Girls Who Are Never Satisfied**
½ cup buckwheat flour
½ cup all-purpose flour
1 tsp. salt
1 tbsp. baking powder
1¼ cups milk (or soy milk, rice milk, etc.)
1 tbsp. melted butter
1 tbsp. sweetener (honey, maple syrup, agave, etc.)

Mix dry ingredients in a large bowl. Set aside. Mix wet ingredients in a smaller bowl, then add to dry ingredients, stirring just enough to combine (lumps are okay). Ladle pancake batter onto a hot skillet. When bubbles appear in the center of the pancake, flip and cook another minute.

Serve with butter, jam, or syrup. Eat slowly and carefully, as pancakes are more powerful than they initially appear. If nothing else satisfies you, these will.

After the breakfast warm-up period, we trooped outside for gardening class. "Class" is a loose designation for what amounts to supervised digging. Today we re-staked tomato plants, picked basil and zucchini, and weeded a carrot patch. I ended up kneeling next to Brooke, watching her smock dress become streaked with dirt and mud as she attacked crabgrass and knotweed. When I asked to borrow her trowel, she ignored me entirely.

When we moved to the zucchini patch, I took the chance to move myself into friendlier territory, setting my things down next to Victoria. Plucking one of the plant's curly tendrils, I held it up next to her curly head. "Check it out," I said. "The plant's imitating your hair."

She blew one of her own curly tendrils out of her face and groaned. "I hate these things. They make my face look fat."

"They do not."

"They do. And I forgot my flat-iron."

I turned to the girl next to me, who happened to be Jane. "Jane, tell Victoria that her adorable, angelic curls do not make her face look fat," I said.

Jane looked up, startled to hear her name. Her eyes flicked

between Victoria and me for an awkward moment until Victoria broke the silence by saying, "Hey, eighty-five percent of men prefer straight hair to curly hair. I rest my case."

Jane didn't respond. Instead, she picked up her trowel and walked quickly away from us to the row of basil plants where Brooke was collecting leaves. I looked at Victoria in puzzlement.

"That was weird," I said.

"She's shy," Victoria said.

"She hates me."

"Why would she hate you? That's crazy," Victoria said. "Look, I found a good one."

She snipped another tendril from the vine and whipped it around in the air. "Why are curly things so funny? Curly pasta, pigs' tails—"

"Slinkies."

"The word *boing*."

We laughed.

"It's true. Curly things are inherently funny."

"Such is my fate," Victoria sighed. "To be a Southern girl with comical hair."

Devon came around with a bucket. "Zoe. Haley. Victoria. Anything to add to the harvest?" she asked.

"Yeah, two," Victoria said, depositing a pair of zucchinis in the bucket.

She waited until Devon was out of earshot and then whispered, "The way she always says our names reminds me of a car salesman."

"Or a cult leader," I added. We mulled over this in silence.

Jane and Brooke, I saw, were conferring as they snipped at the glossy basil plants. I'd heard both of them complain incessantly about gardening class—about the fact that their nails get dirty and their thighs ache—but I know the truth, which is that gardening is their favorite part of the day. Why? Because it burns calories. Gardening is basically a sequence of squats, lifts, and lunges, with pots instead of free weights and weeds instead of rowing machines. It's the only quasi-aerobic activity we're permitted to do. I guarantee that every one of Brooke's movements is calculated to burn the maximum number of breakfast calories. Same thing for Jane.

While I boiled under the sun, I tried to imagine what my mother was doing at home. No doubt relaxing on the porch with a copy of *Artforum* and a glass of mint tea, cool as a cucumber. What does she have to worry about? Nothing, especially now that's she's gotten rid of me for the summer. Had she known that her daughter would be slaving away under the eye of a ponytailed overseer in khaki shorts? Probably. She probably knew exactly what she was signing me up for.

But why?

The question brought my trowel to a freeze halfway through its mound of sun-warmed dirt. I had assumed, over the past four days, that my mother was kept incommunicado simply because my phone and Internet privileges had been yanked away. But what if that weren't the case? What if she were receiving daily updates about my activities and my progress?

That would explain the prickling sense of surveillance that

attends every second of the day here, whether expressed through Devon's hawkish gaze or the creepily ambient sense of being watched.

For the amount of money my mom is forking over, I reasoned, she must be receiving bulletins of some kind. There must be daily phone conferences—or, at the very least, e-mail exchanges. Did the memo say anything about all of this? I must remember to check tonight.

The first thing I'm going to do when I get home is research the possibilities for legally emancipating myself.

When gardening was over, Victoria, Haley, and I commandeered a shady spot opposite the vegetable patch and sprawled out on the grass. We spread our arms wide, encouraging the breeze to dry our sweat. When it's hot out, I become less aware of where my body ends and the air begins. The lines are sharper in winter. In summer, you can blow a stream of air at your wrist and it's no warmer or cooler than the atmosphere, just different.

From our leafy spot we watched the other girls—Jane, Brooke, Caroline—file into the house, out of sight. An hour remained until cooking class and two hours before lunch. I couldn't imagine putting another iota of food into my stomach, which was still busting at the seams with that heavy pancake matter.

"What's she like?" Victoria asked.

"Who?"

"Your roommate. I can't get a handle on her."

"Me neither," I said. "She floats around like a lost electron. I can never tell what she's thinking or where she's going."

"She's the skinniest one here," Haley observed.

"She's rich," I added.

"Rich? She doesn't look rich."

"Don't be fooled. It's a certain kind of rich," I said. "Old money. She's a blue blood—her family goes back to the *Mayflower*."

"Ah."

"Faded polo shirts, hand-me-down pearls, that sort of thing," I elaborated.

"She told me the *Mayflower* thing too," Haley said. "D'you think it's true?"

"Maybe. That's the only personal fact she's shared so far. And I'm her roommate, for God's sake."

"She's probably terrified of you," Victoria said.

"Me? I'm about as scary as an amoeba."

"Don't undersell yourself."

I peered at Victoria, trying to figure out what she meant by that. Victoria met my gaze evenly. Before I could say anything, Haley spoke.

"She does have funny eyes. They're too big for her face."

Victoria nodded vigorously. "You know what she looks like? One of those cat clocks with the moving eyes. What are those called?"

"Kit-Cat Clocks? The ones where the tail moves, too?"

"Yeah. They give me the heebie-jeebies. She looks like one of those."

"Why are we talking about clocks?" Haley complained.

"Because we're bonding," Victoria said. "We're forging connections. It's Group Downtime, and we're healing each other. In a group."

"Blorgh," I said.

Haley plucked a daisy from the lawn. "We could make a daisy chain," she suggested.

"What are you, ten years old?" Victoria said.

"Fine, jeez."

"I'm kidding. What do you think we're making for lunch?" It was a relevant question, since cooking class is generally when we prepare the afternoon meal and sometimes its attendant dessert.

"Zucchini-tomato quinoa with flaxseed?" I guessed. "Curried lentil paté?"

"Hippie food," Victoria said. "I can't get over how retro the menu is here. It's like somebody combined a time capsule from 1965 with astronaut food and then exploded it inside Devon's weird little vegetarian head. Is she from California? She must be from California."

I kept improvising. "Smoky tofu-stuffed peppers with coconut butter? Banana-carob squares?"

"STOP!" Victoria and Haley cried simultaneously.

"Sorry." I said, smiling wickedly. I let a pregnant pause go by, then leaned over and whispered directly in Victoria's ear, "Sprouted wheat-berry loaf."

She shrieked and socked me in the arm.

"On a serious note," I said, "I'm glad we're good enough friends that you feel comfortable beating me."

"Me too. Not bad for—what, five days? Is that how long you've been at this hellhole?"

"Yeah." It was true, too—being thrown together in this way had prompted me to befriend Victoria faster than I'd ever befriended a soul before, except Elise.

Haley looked up from the daisy chain she'd started. "My stomach hurts."

"Mine too, now that I think about it," I said.

"Mine three," Victoria added, rolling over on her elbows. "Probably because I ate dessert last night. I can't even remember the last time I ate dessert."

"Me neither. My mom doesn't like sweets, so the only time I got dessert was if my best friend's parents took us out to dinner," I said. "Once I made the discovery that all restaurant desserts are exactly the same, I quit eating them altogether."

The other two looked at me curiously. "What do you mean, all the same?" Haley asked.

"Dessert menus all follow the same pattern," I explained. "There's always a fruit dessert, a lemon dessert, a chocolate dessert, a cold dessert, and a custard dessert."

"Interesting theory," Victoria observed.

"It applies to every restaurant," I said confidently. "If we had our phones, I could show you ten menus that fit the pattern."

"Give an example," Haley said.

"Okay. A dessert menu at your typical, nice-ish restaurant would be, like, nectarine cobbler, lemon pistachio tart, chocolate mascarpone cake, vanilla bean ice cream, caramel pot de crème. See? All the bases covered."

"I love it," Victoria said. "You're a geek. Just like me. Is that when your food thing started, Zo? With the desserts?"

I paused momentarily at the abruptness of the question. I'd known all along that I'd have to answer a similar question at some point, but I hadn't expected it to come this soon. Not having a ready answer, I deflected the question. "I dunno," I said, turning toward Haley. "When did yours start?"

"God, I remember the moment so well," Haley began. "I could divide my life into 'before' and 'after' categories."

Victoria was nodding in agreement, and I mimicked the gesture. It was crucial for me to blend in at this point. Haley and Victoria might suspect me to be different from the rest of them—my appearance broadcasts this fact like a ticker tape at the New York Stock Exchange—but I certainly didn't need to underscore my wolf-in-sheep's-clothing status.

"After my parents divorced," Haley began, "my dad started a tradition of getting us donuts for breakfast every Friday. We called it Donut Day."

"Creative," Victoria said.

"My brothers and I would tell him what kind of donuts we wanted, and he'd write it all down on a Post-it note. My dad's a dermatologist—very scrupulous. He took the Post-it with him to the donut store to make sure he wouldn't forget anything.

"At first I always got a pink frosted donut. The cake kind, with sprinkles, like a Homer Simpson donut. My brothers got chocolate devil's food donuts and apple strudel sticks, which were somehow the 'cool' donuts." She paused. "It's funny how even *breakfast pastries* get divided into 'cool' and 'lame' categories."

"It's true," I said. "Jelly donuts are so dorky."

"Danishes are the worst," Victoira said. "Someone's dad is always eating a cheese danish and getting crumbs on his shirt. If you order a danish, you're dead."

"So, Donut Day," Haley went on. "My dad would run out and return fifteen minutes later with two brown paper sacks. My brothers would be waiting at the table, drooling, like a pair of mastiffs. My dad poured us all glasses of milk, and himself a cup of coffee, and then we'd rip into the donuts. It never took my brothers longer than four minutes to demolish three donuts apiece—not only because they were starving, but because they were popular and couldn't wait to get to school."

"Ugh," I said, thinking of my own brother. "I know the type."

"Seriously. So obnoxious. Anyhow, there was one day when I didn't have any clean clothes to wear because my dad had, once again, forgotten to do the laundry. Fourth graders aren't old enough to buy their own clothes, but"—she made a face of rueful recollection—"they *are* old enough to make fun of each other for wearing uncool clothes."

"Fourth grade is a minefield," I said.

"Every grade is a minefield," Victoria corrected.

"Yeah," Haley agreed. "So, while my dad was getting breakfast, I dug through the hamper and tried to find a shirt that wasn't stained with chocolate milk or dirty. I was in a panic. By the time I found a passable top and got downstairs, everyone had finished eating and left the table. The table was a mess of napkins, waxed paper, and squashed paper bags. I sat down and rifled through until I found my pink donut. A quarter of it had been amputated, and all the icing was sheared off."

"Aw," I said. "The best part."

Victoria looked wistful, as though she were thinking of her own beloved donuts from the past.

"It looked like someone had given my donut a buzz cut and then stepped on it," Haley said. "Pathetic. I felt pathetic, too, in my dirty shirt. I looked down at the donut, this sad little puck, and realized that I didn't want it after all."

Haley sat up and stretched her shirt over her knees, creating a tent. "Then I thought to myself, *Well, Haley, you need to eat breakfast because lunch isn't until noon and your stomach will growl during class.* So I lifted the donut up to my mouth. But then I put it back down again because another weird thought had occurred to me. *I wonder what would happen,* I thought, *if I didn't eat breakfast.* It started as a sort of experiment. The option of not eating had never occurred to me before."

Despite being uncomfortably full from breakfast, I began to get the first stirrings of a donut craving from listening to Haley's story. Humans are amazingly suggestible. Thoughts of maple icing, crispy fried ridges, and pillowy yellow interiors drifted through my mind. I could almost smell nutmeg and hot oil. But now wasn't the time for donut fantasies. Somehow—quickly—I had to figure out a story to tell.

"It was one of the first independent decisions I made," Haley went on. "And it was intoxicating. I couldn't control much in life, but I could control this. Instead of Donut Day, Fridays became the day that I didn't eat breakfast."

"Were you hungry?" Victoria asked.

"I was. I still *wanted* to eat the donut, but I no longer *needed* to eat the donut."

Haley stretched her nightshirt even tighter over her knees and drew her arms inside for warmth. She resembled a Jujube.

"That's when I first started drawing the distinction between foods that I wanted and foods that I needed," she continued, her chin resting on the taut collar of her shirt. "I did more experiments. When my class went to the cafeteria at lunch, I would eat just one part of my meal—only the chicken fingers, or only the macaroni, for example. One day I'd eat only bread things, which meant my roll and my pizza crust and the croutons in a salad. On another day I'd decide to eat only round things, or only one bite of each thing on my plate, or only yellow things."

"No one noticed?"

She shook her head. "My classmates didn't care, and my parents were too busy. It became my own special, private habit. Something personal and cool, like a toy that I didn't have to share with my brothers or anyone else. It was as though I knew a secret that other people didn't know. The list of foods I wanted got longer and longer, and the list of foods I needed got shorter and shorter."

*I sort of know that feeling,* I thought.

"And the rest . . ." Haley trailed off. "What about you?"

Victoria pursed her doll lips. "I saw it like a game," she said. "Like a crossword puzzle with right answers and wrong answers. And rules. By seventh grade I had the rules down. I had to be 'good' every day except for Saturday. On Saturday I could cheat and eat all the foods I wanted."

"And that worked?" Haley asked.

"It was a psychological trick," Victoria said. "By the time Saturday rolled around, my stomach would be the size of a peanut from eating so little all week, and the fact that I gave myself permission to eat everything made me *not* want to eat everything. It was thrilling, in a weird way."

"It was thrilling because that's the definition of *perversity*," I interjected. "Literally. Perversity means doing something specifically *because* you're not supposed to. In other words, you starved yourself on Saturday specifically *because* you were allowed to eat anything on Saturday."

"Right. Totally," Victoria said. "During the week, I would make lists of all the foods I 'planned' to eat on Saturday, even though I knew that I actually wouldn't eat them. I did it during class. My teachers thought I was taking exhaustive notes, but inside my notebook it was just pages and pages of *Lobster roll, almond croissant, crab cakes with rémoulade, and pommes frites.*"

"I kept mental lists," Haley said. "Mint-chip ice cream, raw cookie dough, garlic bread from one of those foil packages that you put in the oven and the middle comes out raw."

"Chicken paillard," Victoria said. "Dark chocolate broken into shiny squares. Red velvet cake with cream cheese icing."

"Tater tots. Movie popcorn drenched in fake butter."

It was dizzying to watch them go back and forth.

"I want a donut," I said. "The lame kind. With jelly oozing out from the middle."

Both of them turned to me, each having had the same thought. "And you?" Victoria said. "When did yours start?"

"Freshman year," I said, picking a random time frame. I didn't want to sink my brand-new alliances by announcing that I was an imposter who didn't have any reason to be here. I mean, Jesus.

"*Really?*" they both replied in unison.

Shit. Apparently I picked the wrong answer.

"Why?" I asked.

"That's so . . . *recent*," Haley said. "I was ten."

"I was eleven," Victoria chimed in. "But I guess it's different for everyone."

"Eating disorders are all slightly different," Haley nodded.

"Like snowflakes?" I asked.

"Or thumbprints."

"Or genetic diseases," Victoria said.

I needed to change the subject, so I lay down on my back and moaned, feigning an even worse stomachache than I had. It worked: Victoria and Haley frowned in sympathy, and Haley instructed me to roll up like a pill bug—"I swear," she said, "it squeezes the pain right out."

I followed her instructions, trying to temper the nervous storm brewing in the back of my mind. I knew that I'd be expected to share the full version of my own story, too, at some point—and then what would I say, except that I'd never had a real problem with food and that I didn't belong here at all? I need to have friends here, but I can't get too close to them. I can't let them ask me about my past. How could I even start to explain?

The truth is that a small fraction of me is able to identify with their battles. I lost some weight last year—a lot of weight, to be precise. But I lost mine in the way anyone loses weight—and in the way that Elise lost weight—which was by eating slightly less and exercising slightly more. I am not even as skinny as the *average* model. And I certainly wasn't refusing breakfast in fourth grade.

But time was on my side this morning. Before either of my friends could dig further for my detailed personal history, Devon emerged in the doorway to call us in for cooking class. We brushed the grass from our legs and trundled over to the front stairs of the house.

"Taco quinoa casserole," Devon announced as we filed inside. I couldn't imagine a more repulsive combination of words.

After cooking and lunch (verdict: even more repulsive than anticipated), I arrived early for my session with Alexandra and took a seat outside her office. The day was halfway over, and already I had divided it into Good and Bad categories. The Good category contained one item, which was that I'd further solidified my friendships with Haley and Victoria. That deserved a gold star. The Bad category, unfortunately, was more numerous. One, I couldn't get the dirt out from beneath my fingernails, and the dark half-moons were a visual annoyance each time I looked down at my hands. Two, I screwed up my minted zucchini soup in cooking class by forgetting to peel the vegetables. While the other girls produced silky, pale emulsions, mine turned a bilious green color, like a blended toad. Three, I could tell that I was starting to gain weight. *As long as I don't gain too much, I can lose it by the time school starts up again.*

Slouching into the chair, I ran a finger lengthwise along my thigh. Viewed from this angle, the contours weren't flattering. What if I didn't have enough time to lose the weight by September? There's little in life that pains me more than the idea of returning to school in worse shape than I left it. There's always one guy who comes back with overdue braces and one girl who comes back chubby. People talk.

Just a few days ago, my body was running as smoothly as a machine. I'd gotten it down to a science, only to be snatched up and dumped into a place designed to reverse my hard-won habits. The timing could not have been worse: I'd beaten the odds and lost weight. I'd kept myself decently skinny for a whole year. I was still a giant compared to waif-like Elise, but still. And now this. If it is possible for a person's brain to cringe, that's what mine does every time my tongue locates some forgotten crumb of Twin Birch breakfast stuck between my back teeth.

I shoved these complaints out of my mind and referred to the wall clock. Five minutes to go. The red lacquered box sat next to me on its wicker table, same as before. Since that first session with Alexandra, I've adopted a habit of peeking inside the box, just out of curiosity. It was empty the first time I checked, but it hasn't been empty since. And as I stood today to look through the slit at the top of the box, an obscure part of me wished that it would be empty once more. It wasn't.

I straightened up and sat back down. One minute to go. When I initially asked Alexandra what the box was for, I thought her explanation sounded very queer. I still do, but the oddness is touched with a glimmer of logic.

For the next sixty seconds I let my mind wander to golden Oreos, V-neck T-shirts, and Coney Island, in that order. Random things.

"Hello, Zoe," I heard from beside me.

Alexandra's door was open. She stood smiling, her black bob glossier than a licorice jellybean. It reminded me of an actress from the 1920s whose name I couldn't summon. Lulu something? I wished that I had my phone back. It would take all of three seconds to Google the actress. Problems that a split second of Internet research would solve are arising here as a daily source of irritation. The lack of Googling privileges is another bothersome aspect of finding oneself locked away from the world.

"Water? Tea?" Alexandra offered. She wore her usual outfit of white pants and tunic, but without the scarf or costume jewelry I'd come to expect. Her uniform, I should note, follows a distinct pattern: All of her garments are white with the exception of a single splotch of color. It's the same every time. White, white, white, and then a dab of brightness—never more than one—by way of a red headband or an electric-blue shoe. Secretly, I looked forward to seeing where the color pops up each day. It's a private game for me to play, like a treasure hunt. Another way to distract myself.

Today's accessory was a pair of poppy-orange flats that were pointy at the toe. They reminded me of traffic cones.

I declined the offer of a drink.

"What's on your mind today?" Alexandra asked, after we'd arranged ourselves on the chair and couch respectively.

"Tricks."

"Tricks?"

"Yeah. For eating," I said. "Did you know that Haley used to slice grapes into slivers to make them last longer? She told me all about her strategies during breakfast. So did Victoria. *Grape slivers.*"

"Hmm," Alexandra said.

"And Victoria set her alarm for five a.m. so she could run for an hour before school," I went on. "Then, she did the same thing *after* school every single day. Two runs of four miles each. Her rule was that she ate all of her food for the day before eight a.m., so she had time to burn it off.

"She ate the same thing every day, which was a protein shake that she made in the blender with almond milk and peanut butter. She drank it after her morning run, intentionally swallowing it fast so that the protein powder would expand in her stomach and make her queasy. The queasiness would stop her from eating anything else for the rest of the day."

As I relayed these things to Alexandra, I marveled at my ability to perfectly recall the details of the conversation I'd had the day before. Unlike most things, Victoria and Haley's tricks remained vivid in my mind, down to the flavor (cookies and cream) of Victoria's protein powder.

"After a while," I continued, "she started dreaming about protein shakes at night. She woke up with drool on her pillow from anticipating the shake. And when she went on her first run, that's all she thought about: the cold, frosty breakfast that lay ahead."

"Hmm," said Alexandra.

"And Haley—holy crap. Haley was even worse. At the beginning of the week, she'd buy seven containers of low-fat rice pudding and mark them with a Sharpie: *M* for *Monday*, *T* for *Tuesday*, *W* for *Wednesday*. Then she'd steam up a batch of vegetables and portion those out into seven plastic Tupperware containers, one for each day. She'd put those in the fridge with the pudding. And then she took seven Ziploc bags and put, in each one, ten cashews, ten pretzels, and two rice cakes. Every day of the week she would eat a rice pudding for breakfast and a container of vegetables for dinner. For the rest of the day, she carried the Ziploc bag around and nibbled from it."

"You find these details interesting," Alexandra observed.

"Don't you?" I said. "Obsessiveness is fascinating."

"How come?"

"For the same reason that anything is fascinating. Because it's different."

"But Zoe," Alexandra said, "I'm not so sure that it *is* different."

"How do you mean?"

"When I spoke to your mother, she mentioned that you and Elise developed some restrictive eating habits."

"When did you speak to my mother?" I asked, my voice unexpectedly sharp. One look at Alexandra's face was enough to tell me that she wouldn't divulge the information, so I waved my own question away. "Never mind. But you can't compare Elise and me to these girls. There's a huge difference in our situations."

"What's that?"

"We *ate*. The difference is that Elise and I ate."

Alexandra made a note on the legal pad in her lap, then trained her eyes back on me. "It sounds as though you ate little and controlled your diet strictly, Zoe. You controlled your intake to the point where it became a source of concern to those who cared about you."

"Losing weight isn't the same as anorexia," I rebutted, repeating the same point I'd made before. This was exasperating. "You know what? It really annoys me when adults pretend not to see subtleties. Just because a teenage girl wants to drop five pounds, doesn't mean she needs to be incarcerated at a clinic."

"That's true," said Alexandra. "When we left off yesterday, we were talking about your mother. And your feelings of anger toward her."

"Well, I don't feel too angry anymore."

"That's good, Zoe. Why?"

"I don't know. The anger sort of turned into frustration, and then the frustration lost momentum."

She nodded. "Anger is an exhausting emotion. I'm glad you allowed yourself to feel angry instead of stifling it."

"Gardening helped. I was violent with the pigweed."

"That's a good way to metabolize the anger."

"It was a real bloodbath." I held up my dirty nails as proof. "I thought about writing my mother a letter, but I didn't."

"Why not?"

"I don't know."

"You've written letters to Elise," Alexandra said. It was a statement without a question mark, and the quicksilver change of subject threw me off balance. While I struggled to think of a response, Alexandra continued. "I'd love to talk about Elise today."

"Okay," I said slowly. My voice sounded raw, as though it had been sanded down a layer.

"I understand that you miss her very much."

"Yes," I said. "I think about her every minute. It's the worst part of being here."

The sofa beneath me began to tremble. An earthquake? No. It was my thighs that were shaking. I pushed my shoes hard against the ground in order to steady them, but a tiny vibration was still evident. I hoped it wasn't visible from Alexandra's vantage.

"I keep thinking about all the stuff she's probably doing at home while I'm here," I said.

"Such as?"

"Walking in Central Park. Taking photos. Picking mint leaves from her backyard, squeezing lemons into iced tea. Making popsicles."

An endless, expectant minute passed before Alexandra responded. Did she assume that I was having deep thoughts during these pauses? Because I was not. My mind was blank.

"Have you told the other girls here about your friendship with Elise?"

"No."

"Why not?"

"Because I haven't told anyone anything."

"What about Caroline?"

"Caroline? She's the last person I'd talk to. No," I corrected myself, "that's not true—Brooke is the last person I'd talk to. Caroline is the runner-up."

"How come?"

"She's like an egg. She rolls around in her shell, saying nothing and doing nothing. An empty surface. I have no idea how to talk to her." Pause. "And I've tried." (This wasn't terribly true, but I didn't want Alexandra to think me a misanthrope.)

"Caroline is shy. But I have a feeling it might make you feel better to reach out to her. She could be a wonderful resource."

"Resource," I echoed. "You make it sound like she's an oil well."

"And I know she feels the same way about you."

"Somehow I doubt this."

"You can be an intimidating person, Zoe."

"Oh, come on," I said. "I have more social anxiety than anyone I know. When I started kindergarten, my mom had to put me in bed for an hour every day after school because I was so overwhelmed by the presence of other people that I felt physically sick. Intimidating is the last thing that I am."

"Roommates are paired very attentively here," Alexandra said.

"Meaning?"

"Meaning Caroline is your roommate for a reason."

I sat with this.

"Who decides?" I asked.

"Angela and myself."

Of course. My question had been idiotic. *Think before speaking*, I commanded myself.

"I'd love to see you get to know Caroline a little," Alexandra said. "And of course I'll be encouraging her to do the same."

"Fine," I said.

"You could talk to her about Elise. That might be a good place to start."

"I have, actually. Once." The conversation had been so brief and unproductive that I'd almost erased it from my mind.

"And—?"

"On the second day, she asked about a photo I had. A picture of Elise and me from the first day of sophomore year. It was a cell phone picture that I printed out."

"And what did she ask you?"

"She asked who the picture was of, and I told her. I think she was annoyed that her ten perfect picture frames were no longer the centerpiece of the room. I don't know what the deal is with those pictures, but she is *very* protective over them. Did you know that she polish—"

"Let's stay on your conversation," Alexandra interrupted. "How did Caroline respond when you told her about Elise?"

"She turned off the lamp and went to sleep sucking her thumb."

Alexandra scribbled something else on her legal pad.

"As conversations go," I summarized, "it was pretty much a nonstarter."

The angle of the legal pad—balanced on Alexandra's leg and canted away from my eyes—made it impossible to tell what she'd written, and the secrecy of her notes unsettled me. There's something inherently taunting about a therapist's notepad. Indeed, when any object is "off-limits"—when you're prohibited from seeing or touching it—it takes on an evil, threatening aura.

"Why is this important?" I asked uneasily. "What are you writing?"

"I'd love to come back to all of this in detail, but we're out of time. Perhaps you could drop by later today before dinner? It would be wonderful to touch base before our appointment tomorrow. I think we're on a good track."

"I don't know," I said, plucking a stray thread from my leggings, which still trembled. "I wanted to write Elise a letter today."

I examined the thread and dropped it on the ground, where it formed a stark black line against the white carpet.

"How about this," Alexandra suggested, capping her pen. "We'll hold off until your session tomorrow to address the topics we broached today. But today, for a change, I'd like you to mix with Caroline during Group Downtime instead of spending the time with Victoria and Haley."

(How did she know what I did during Group Downtime?)

The thought of socializing with Caroline turned my stomach into a raisin, but I signaled agreement with a passive nod. What else could I do?

"Think of it as a fun assignment," Alexandra said, standing to open her office door for me. With her shimmering black hair, sleek top, and witchy flats, she looked less like a therapist than the executive of a lifestyle TV channel. I didn't get it.

As I started down the hallway, I heard her call out softly.

"Oh, and Zoe?"

I swiveled around. Alexandra leaned out of her doorway.

"How are you feeling about our agreement?" she asked.

I thought of the white cardstock box that Alexandra had

given me during our first session. I stored the box beneath my bed, out of sight. But always within reach.

"Fine," I said. "It's going fine."

"Good."

I waited for more questions, but none came.

"Have fun with Caroline today," she added, with a small wave. "Tomorrow you can tell me all about it."

*Right,* I thought. *Tomorrow.*

Dear Elise,

Day six. When I zoom out to consider the fact that I'll be here for thirty-six days—the length of a standard summer camp session—my mind turns into an iTunes visualizer. All productive thoughts halt and my brainspace fills up with imploding swirlies, dots, and abstract fireworks. No music, though. Just unaccompanied chaos.

Want to know how many pounds I've gained?

That's a trick question. I have no clue how many pounds I've gained because one of the novel aspects of the Twin Birch treatment is that we are not weighed. We are not asked to strip to our underwear and stand atop a cold doctor's scale. We are not forced to watch in terror as the number climbs, ounce by ounce, pound by pound, with each passing day. There is no last-minute chugging of water or hiding of weights in our underwear before the weigh-in. None of this petty deception is permitted at Twin Birch.

Instead, we are provoked to speculate about our "progress." And there is plenty of time to do so.

When Alexandra first told me that I would not be weighed, I nodded and asked no questions. What was there to ask about? I could easily guess the reasoning behind the no-weighing rule: people with eating disorders, for all their supposed deficiencies, are spectacularly good at math. And while I'm far from anorexic, I've spent enough time among these other girls that their numerical prowess has rubbed off on me. Like them, I can easily calculate the number of calories on my plate, the number of calories burned off during gardening class, and the number of calories extinguished by my basal metabolism. I have a running number in my head as long as a grocery receipt. I know how many calories are in a plum (40) and how many calories are in a cup of the thick Greek yogurt that we eat for breakfast (220), and how many are in a quarter cup of the deceptively fibrous-looking granola that we are urged to sprinkle on top of that yogurt (250). This is a minuscule sample of the information now stored in my head. Name any kind of food and I'll tell you how many calories are in a tablespoon, a handful, or a scoop. My mother would be displeased to know that my mind is filled with such facts. If brainpower is a zero-sum operation, a huge amount of algebra and European history is being deleted to make room for the nutritional rundown of, say, six ounces of pineapple (85 calories, 17 grams sugar, 22 grams carbohydrates, zero fat). After this is all over, she'll wish she sent me to a public high school.

On the brighter side, a single day spent at Twin Birch would swiftly disprove the old stereotype that girls have inferior math skills to boys. Given the speed at which caloric numbers are added, divided, and multiplied here, that cliché can't possibly be true.

So the question remains: How much weight have I gained?

Well, I can't give you an exact figure. Without a scale to spit out the digits, the number remains relative.

For example, I have gained more weight than Caroline and less weight than Haley.

I have gained enough weight to produce a small ripple of fat that spills over my leggings when I pull them on in the morning.

I have not gained enough weight to see cellulite appear on my thighs.

I have gained enough weight that my ribs are less visible when I lift my arms in the air.

But not totally invisible.

I have gained enough weight to see my upper arms thicken.

I have not gained as much weight as my mother would like me to gain.

When I dispatch these statistics, I wonder what you

are thinking. Are you worried? Disappointed? It isn't easy to write any of it down, you know. When I write out, on paper, that I've put on weight, my instinct is to scratch out the offending sentence and start over again with a new one. But if I did that, would anything change? No. I'd simply be back at square one, writing the same sentence again. I have gained weight. I have gained weight. I have gained weight.

My mind returns to the subject of my mother. Is there a number that she would like me to hit? And if so, what is that number? When she was deciding whether or not to mail out the application for Twin Birch, did she watch me carefully, promising herself that she would stamp and send the envelope if I dipped below X number or Y number of pounds? Being here has prompted me to look back over the past few months with a vigilant eye. I review old incidents, trying to figure out whether I was auditioning, inadvertently, for a spot at Twin Birch. I curse myself for every egg-white omelet I ordered or sliver of avocado I refused to eat in front of her. I should have been more careful about hiding my habits.

But back to the question of math. Re-reading what I've written so far in this letter, I worry that I'm being too abstract in my explanation of the circumstances here. So I will give you concrete examples of this math business. I will "show my work."

Breakfast today. Imagine a dining room bathed in a bright morning sunshine that starkly illuminates each platter of food. Today those platters contained cornmeal pancakes, each one modest—the size of a softball—but soon to be stacked high on our plates, the way pancakes are stacked in cartoons. Filagreed dishes contain our choice of toppings: honey butter (70 calories per tablespoon), maple syrup (200 calories per quarter cup), peaches sauteed in butter (150), a scoop of heavy whipped cream (250) from a tureen kept on ice. Don't forget the handful of honey-roasted pecans (280) scattered on top. And the pancakes themselves? Only, according to Victoria's calculations, 180 calories each—but we're served six of them.

There's coffee too, of course. Coffee has zero calories, but we're only allowed one cup.

That adds up to roughly 1,100 calories before nine o'clock, if you eat the bare minimum required of you. To make matters harder, Alexandra occasionally sits in on breakfast and take notes on her legal pad, which means that I am scrutinized not only by Devon, and not only by the other five girls, but by my therapist, who is no doubt analyzing my intake and tucking the results into a folder somewhere. Sometimes I fantasize about stealing the notepad from Alexandra's hands and reading it. What could she possibly be writing? *8:14 a.m.: Patient examines single banana slice, displaying contempt (or possibly hesitation). Patient stabs fruit with fork. Symbolic gesture?*

As we picked at and deconstructed our pancakes this morning, I was reminded of the fact that I weigh at least ten pounds more than the second-biggest girl here. I may be skinny, but my hair is not brittle like Caroline's, and my thighs don't resemble a wishbone like Haley's.

Still, nobody will tell me why I'm here.

After breakfast, Devon led us into the living room to warm up. As usual, I was not particularly cold. Caroline and Jane had started watching a DVD of Hitchcock's *Rear Window* last night, and they asked Devon if they could finish the movie during warm-up. She said sure, if it was okay with everyone else. Everyone else nodded, and Jane slid the DVD into its player. Grace Kelly popped up onscreen.

*I wish I were creative,* she was saying.

*You are,* said the Jimmy Stewart character. *You're great at creating difficult situations.*

I quickly zoned out. My attention span is exactly the length of a TV show, not a movie. I can never focus on a whole movie unless I'm doing something with my hands at the same time, like folding laundry. On either side of me, Victoria and Haley watched the movie attentively, wrapped up in a scene where Grace Kelly bustles about in a full-skirted wasp-waist dress. I watched the actress cross the screen and wondered briefly if she was anorexic. Her waist was tiny. Other than that, the movie was dull as dust, and I had to fight the impulse to get up and move around. The feeling of entrapment was reinforced by Devon, whose supervision had the quality of a prison-tower guard.

I picked at the silk upholstery of the couch, my mood

darkening as I unraveled stray threads. The elegance of Twin Birch, I thought, is a sham. It is elegant because it constricts its inhabitants. It's like a corset in this way. The laces may be sewn of satin, but the cinching is rib-breakingly painful. I'd much rather be in a prison than in a prison disguised as a family estate. At least with the former, you know what you're getting into.

My feet tapped impatiently against the floor. Nothing had happened so far in the movie—its plot was moving forward at the rate of spilled molasses. I wasn't cold, and I didn't need to warm up. Boredom engulfed me like a noxious fog. I couldn't stand the stillness any longer.

"Devon?" I asked impulsively, interrupting the movie. Several turned to look at me. "Can I go to the bathroom?"

"Sure," Devon said. She looked around the room expectantly, waiting for someone to volunteer. After mealtimes we're required to have a companion go with us to the bathroom, to ensure that we don't throw up our food. I looked to Victoria, who was my default companion, wondering why she hadn't instantly popped up to accompany me. My stomach sank. Victoria and Haley were nestled against each other, dozing. Why had they picked *this* moment to take a nap? Victoria had never failed to be my bathroom partner. I turned back just as Devon pointed to Caroline. "Why don't you two partner up?" she said.

Caroline looked displeased, but she couldn't say no to the request. She stood with a wobble and followed me to

the door as Brooke and Jane exchanged glances. *Great*—
I didn't even have to go to the bathroom. I'd planned to
get my ya-yas out by doing a few sets of lunges across the
bathroom floor. Now what? Caroline's mouse-like footsteps echoed my own as we walked down the hallway. The
situation, I realized, at least presented me with a decent
opportunity to follow through on Alexandra's prescription. But what could I possibly say to Caroline?

I slowed my pace, hoping that she'd catch up and walk
beside me. Instead, she slowed her own pace as soon as
she realized what I was doing. Clever. As we got to the
bathroom door, I turned around to say something—anything!—in hopes of starting a brief and perfunctory conversation. There was no chance to do so. As I turned, a
high-pitched rattle noise escaped from Caroline's mouth.
She jumped back a foot in surprise—had I turned too
suddenly?—and shrank from my presence like prey
from a lion. I gawked at her, unable to process her reaction. Surprise turned to shame. She made me feel like
a monster, regarding me with eyes that were absolutely
soaked in fear. I pushed open the bathroom door, closed
it behind me, and turned on the faucet. Hot with shame
and confusion, I held my wrists beneath the cold water as
Caroline hovered outside. I peered at myself in the mirror, wondering what was so fearsome about me. You never
felt that way, did you?

I hope you will tell me the honest truth.

By now you've had plenty of time to write me back,

Elise, and I'm worried. I'm afraid that something is wrong. Please reply as quickly as you can, even if it's just to send a postcard.

I'll be waiting for it.

From,
Zoe

# [day seven]

*"Can I ask you something?"*

It was Caroline. The lights were out, and the moon threw a pool of milk-hued light onto the bedroom floor. Curled in a fetal position beneath her bedding, she had appeared to be asleep. Not a single word had been spoken since our bewildering encounter outside the bathroom. What time was it?

"Sorry?" I said. (What I really wanted to ask: How did you know I was awake?)

Part of me was relieved that she'd started a conversation with me, even if it was in the dead of night. Perhaps she *wasn't* afraid of me after all—perhaps our earlier experience was a fluke.

Caroline, however, had no intention of following up on that subject.

"This is a question with no judgment implied," she said, barely whispering the words. Her body didn't move beneath the sheets.

"Okay," I replied.

"Why are you here?"

The words met my mind with a thud. They were not what I expected.

"It's a simple question," Caroline added.

We lay in our respective beds, facing each other like parentheses in the dimness.

"Well?" Caroline persisted, her feeble voice growing agitated. The question—combined with the fact that she'd never spoken so much at one time before—momentarily baffled me. Then I almost started to laugh. My first reaction, when attacked, is to laugh. I don't know why.

"I don't know what to tell you," I began, smothering the nervous giggle that threatened to escape.

That much was true: I have no idea what I'm doing here, and at the time I had no clue what her question was supposed to mean. Was it literal? Figurative? Clinical? Or simply designed to make me feel weird? She waited, still as a lizard, for a more satisfying answer.

"You weigh more than Jane," Caroline continued. "I'm trying to understand why someone who clearly isn't at risk of an eating disorder is at a treatment center for anorexics."

I squinted to see her face, but it was too dark. I could only see outlines. Now I knew why she'd waited until the middle of the night to interrogate me. It's much easier to attack a person when you can't see her.

"I'm sorry to be blunt," she went on, still motionless, "but this isn't a personal issue. So don't take it as a personal issue. I don't understand why you're here, and it's starting to bother me."

"Join the goddamn club," I whispered back. "I'm sorry to disappoint you, but I have no clue why I'm here either."

"I asked Alexandra."

"About me?" I asked.

"She wouldn't tell me anything," Caroline said.

*Me either*, I thought. *She wouldn't tell me anything either.* Caroline's questions were evoking in me what must be every rational person's worst fear, which is being asked to justify your existence.

"You must have done something," Caroline said. "I sleep two feet away from you every night—I deserve to know."

Her words turned to bile inside of me. *I must have done something.*

But what? What had I done?

"I'm sorry," I said, swallowing the acid in my throat. "You're not the only one without a clue what I'm doing here."

Silence.

"Believe me," I added more forcefully. "I want to know more than you do."

"I doubt that," Caroline said, flipping over so that her back faced me. The conversation, I gathered, was over.

# [Day Eight]

*One week at Twin Birch is done. Finished.*

Crickets scream from the trees outside as I write. The summer bullfrogs sound like a hundred boys burping in chorus, and my stomach echoes the animal din with its own sonic protests from breakfast, which I forced down after spending a restless night grappling with Caroline's inquiries—it was impossible, of course, to sleep after our conversation. Our seating arrangements at mealtimes have been flexible until now, with Haley sometimes sitting at Jane's table and Caroline taking the seat next to Victoria occasionally. Last night's exchange was a line drawn in the sand—from the moment Caroline turned away, I knew that the factions at Twin Birch were set in stone. On one side is me, Victoria, and Haley. On the other side is Brooke, Jane, and Caroline. From now on, there are no neutral parties.

The only area in which this proves to be a problem is cooking class. To wit: Victoria and Haley are roommates, so they automatically partner up. Brooke and Jane are also roommates, so they automatically partner up. Which leaves—you guessed it—Caroline and me to chop plums and chiffonade basil in acrimonious silence. That's what happened today, and unless somebody dies or disappears, I don't see how it will change.

After a pleasant morning spent batting gnats away and turning our fingernails into filthy crescents in the garden, we gathered in the kitchen to prepare tonight's dessert: a plum galette.

"A galette is meant to be rough around the edges," Devon instructed us as we sliced fruit. "It doesn't need to be perfect."

I rolled out an almond crust while Caroline tossed plums in sugar, standing as far as possible away from me. In the past week, I've learned that girls with eating disorders tend toward fanatical precision when it comes to food. This applies double to baking, which—unlike cooking—is a precise science. Girls with a history of disordered eating excel, in general, at tasks that require precision. What seems like a behavioral defect in one context becomes an asset in the other: Every ounce of flour must be portioned out, every drop of vanilla extract budgeted correctly. Victoria would be a shoo-in pastry chef hire at any four-star restaurant, given that she can eyeball the difference between two and three ounces of sugar at fifty yards. Whenever we work alone rather than in partners, my baked goods turn out poorly. Yesterday's class yielded five perfect onion tarts and one that resembled a chewed frisbee. Guess which one was mine.

Practically everywhere I look, I see evidence that I don't belong here.

In the mirror, I see that I'm thin but not ghastly thin like the other girls.

In the living room, I digest my meals without wrapping myself in a blanket.

In the kitchen, I level a cup of flour without spending ten minutes on the process.

As we assembled our galette today, I thought about what I would tell Alexandra about Caroline. "I tried," I imagined myself telling her during our session. "First she shrunk, and then, later that night, she attacked me. She said that I didn't belong here. She won't talk to me at all—what am I supposed to do?"

Yes, that's what I would tell Alexandra. I had been right about Caroline all along: She wasn't somebody I could trust or talk to. Alexandra would have to admit that she was wrong. *That*, at least, was going to be satisfying.

I was almost excited for today's therapy session.

While I patched the sticky almond dough together, Caroline focused neurotically on arranging her slices in concentric circles. Her hands were splashed in red plum juice, and the galette looked murderously unappetizing.

Caroline sprinkled sugar over the plums with her fingertips. She paused, bit a red-stained nail, and adjusted one plum by five degrees. Our galette was so symmetrical it looked computer-generated. (I hate the word *galette*, by the way. What's wrong with *tart*? *Galette* sounds like a French-Canadian team sport.) It was awful to sit next to Caroline, imagining the mean thoughts she was having about me. Spite was written all over her taut, sour face. She'd even scraped her hair into a tight bun that mirrored her expression.

The ovens beeped, signaling that they had preheated to the proper temperature. Ours was ready to bake, but no one else had finished arranging, so we waited like a pair of statuettes. Torture. I fidgeted, tugged on my cuffs, picked lint from my leggings. I licked my finger, picked up a crumb of crust, and touched it to my tongue. The morsel filled my mouth with a buttery taste, and I regretted it immediately.

Devon clapped for attention. "Everyone ready to bake?" she asked.

"Yes," everyone said, in that deadpan drone that kindergarteners use for performing rote memorization tasks.

"Neato," she said. "It's time to put our little fruity friends in the oven. Follow me."

Caroline lifted our galette and slid from her stool while the others mobilized to deposit their creations and clean up their workstations. I stayed put, watching as four frail wrists wrapped unused butter sticks and replaced them in the refrigerator, followed by four skinny arms sweeping nude plum pits into the compost bin.

"Pretty," Devon said, commenting on Caroline's plum arrangement.

There was sugar all over our table, which I desultorily gathered into a tidy pile. My impulse was to lick my finger again and have a taste, but I resisted. When Caroline returned, she shifted her stool so that her back was to my face. That's me: the perennial social leper. The knife-sharp blades of her shoulders poked right through the Lilly Pulitzer dress she wore.

I stared at the pile of sugar, noting that it resembled a burial mound I'd once seen in *National Geographic*. I wished I could shrink to the size of an ant, burrow inside the sugar mountain, and disappear from sight.

A sudden presence at my elbow made me flinch.

"Zoe! Sorry, didn't mean to scare you." It was Devon.

She knelt. She is always kneeling.

"How're you doing?" she asked.

"Fine."

"You look a little down."

I made a noncommital noise.

"Wanna chat?" she asked, ponytail bobbing. Sometimes it bobs on its own, like a prehensile monkey tail. If I stare at the ponytail long enough, I develop an urge to snip it off with a pair of scissors.

"No thanks. I'm seeing Alexandra after lunch."

"Alrighty. Totally understand. Just yank me aside if you wanna talk about anything during lunch, okay?"

"Okay."

She returned to the front of the class, where she continued to look a bit too often in my direction while talking about the therapeutic value of cooking. I did my best to ignore her glances.

"The goal is to overcome our fears and aversions," Devon was saying, as though rolling marzipan were an FDA-approved prescription. I thought of the cooking class passage I'd memorized from the Twin Birch memo:

*Cooking class is the Twin Birch way of encouraging girls with eating disorders to spend time around food: touching it, smelling it, preparing it, honoring and savoring it.*

I've been returning to the bathroom almost nightly to read

through the memo. When I initially read the cooking section, the first thing that came to mind was a phrase asserting the opposite effect: *Familiarity breeds contempt.*

Part of cooking therapy involves "Mindfulness exercises," like the episode with the apricot. These exercises happen every other day, and they are so meditative (read: excruciatingly boring) that I can't even bring myself to document them in this journal. It's the same deal each time, but with different foods: Devon narrates while we spend ten minutes eating a small morsel and waiting for the experience to become profound.

It doesn't. Not for me.

The smell of baked almond crust began to spread throughout the kitchen, stirring involuntary murmurs from my stomach. I traced the gaudy whirls of Caroline's dress with my eyes in soft focus, as though a Magic Eye pattern might emerge. I felt like I didn't belong, and that it was somehow my fault. I felt as though I were about to break in half.

How will I survive? I barely made it through freshman year alive, and then I had Elise to lean on.

At Twin Birch, I'm on my own.

**Plum Galette for Solitary Girls**
Pastry dough for a pie
7 tbsp. granulated sugar
1 tsp. cinnamon
¼ tsp. nutmeg
Zest of one lemon
6 plums, cut into wedges

Heat oven to 375 degrees. Line a baking sheet with parchment. Form the dough into a 12-inch circle and put it on the baking sheet. Toss the plums with sugar, cinnamon, nutmeg, and lemon zest. Arrange the plums over the dough. Sprinkle a little more sugar on top. Fold the edges of the dough over about an inch to cover the outer edge of plums. Crimp the edges with your fingers to make it look like an illustration in a children's book. Cover the whole thing loosely with foil, bake 40 minutes, remove the foil, and bake a few more minutes. Take the galette out, let it cool, and serve with a glug of cold heavy cream.

This recipe tastes best if you make and eat it by yourself.

Today's meals:

**Breakfast**
Apple-cucumber juice (8 oz.)
Steel-cut oatmeal with almonds and dates

**Lunch**
Avocado-grapefruit salad with cilantro lime dressing (1 cup)
Linguine (1 cup) with sautéed zucchini, garlic, and olive oil
Sourdough bread (1 piece)

**Dinner**
Smoky pumpkin soup with white beans (2 cups)
Lentil salad with garden herbs (½ cup)
Grilled peaches with *fromage blanc* and basil (*didn't eat)

# [day nine]

*I felt a dash of righteous indignation* during therapy yesterday when I told Alexandra about my interactions with Caroline. She was surprised, though I can't imagine why she thought Caroline would be nice to me. "I can read people," I told her. "From the day I got here, I knew Caroline didn't like me." Alexandra wasn't satisfied with this, but I was eager to address another topic during our fifty-minute session, and she reluctantly agreed to move on. What I wanted to talk about had happened only an hour earlier, at lunch.

Until midday, nothing unusual had occurred. At a place like this, where routines are paramount and every minute of every hour is allotted for a specific purpose, aberrations are rare. When they happen, they are viewed as bloopers to be smoothed over as speedily as possible. But what happened last night—and what we learned about this afternoon—will not be so easily erased from the record.

Lunchtime. We sat grimly before watermelon-fennel salad and lentil tamales, the air quiet except for the sound of knives scraping reluctantly against plates. Lunch is the hardest meal of the day for me; somehow, when I go to bed each night, I make myself believe that the next day will be a new start. That I'll wake up in my own bed, with my own walls surrounding me, and my phone within reach. That I'll pop up and shower for as long as I want, brew my own cup of English Breakfast just the way I like it—nice and strong, tiny splash of skim milk, no sugar. When I open my eyes each day to the racket of Devon banging her wake-up bell, therefore, it is not only disheartening but shocking. At breakfast, I'm still too sleep-dazed to think clearly. By lunchtime, the realization has truly sunk in.

The midday meal is correspondingly grueling. Lunchtime is when I resign myself to the reality of a day spent feeling like a foie gras duck: stuffed, caged, and disgusting. Dinner is manageable only because I know that I'll be unconscious soon, and therefore incapable of regretting every bite.

Today I was delighted to find an element of the meal that I could actually—*gasp!*—enjoy. The watermelon had been chilled and carved into precise cubes, and the rectilinearity of the fruit was appealing to me in the same way that plastic sushi is appealing. Even piled up in a big bowl, I could tell that the melon cubes were all the same size, and a cube is much easier to eat than a big pile of mush. The mint was from the garden. I finished mine in less than twenty minutes, which is a record around here. After I finished, I sat with my glass of iced tea and suffered through the spiteful rumbles and moans of my stomach. My tablemates ate slowly: Victoria stabbed her tamale à la Norman Bates in *Psycho*; Haley palpated hers like a doctor checking for tumors. There were complaints.

"This is revolting," Victoria said, holding a glob of lentil paste up to the light. "I want saltines with apple jelly. That's all I want to eat."

Apple jelly is a Southern thing. Victoria talks about it a lot.

"We're eating a corn pouch stuffed with pulverized beans," she went on. "If that isn't gross, I don't know what is."

"Mayonnaise?" Haley suggested.

"Mayonnaise is gross, too."

"And lobster?" Haley added. "Did you know that lobsters are technically insects? Giant insects from the sea that people eat?"

We were hashing out this point when Angela showed up in the doorway. This was unexpected—her rare appearances in the dining room always coincided with breakfast, when she occasionally checked in with Devon. Devon seemed equally surprised to see the head administrator upstairs at lunch, and she hurried over with an anxious look, brushing tamale crumbs from her shorts.

Devon didn't even bother to clap for attention before making the announcement.

"Lunch is over," she announced, after whispering with Angela. "Everyone into the living room."

Victoria, Haley, and I glanced at one another with eyebrows raised. Something was up.

At the next table, Caroline smiled triumphantly. When I looked at her plate, I could see why: She hadn't eaten one bite of her meal, and now she wouldn't have to consume even a token crumb.

We filed into the living room, where Angela now stood by the unlit fire, her hands folded stiffly across her chest. Next to her sat Brooke, whose eyes were red with tears behind the wire-rimmed glasses. Brooke, I now realized, had been absent at lunch. I wondered why I had been slightly more relaxed than usual.

We found seats and arranged ourselves in a semicircle. Brooke, wearing a black dress flecked with bits of her breakfast, simmered in her chair, eyes flickering between me, Victoria, and Haley. Before Angela could begin, Brooke stood up and addressed the three of us.

"One of you did it," she said. "I know it was one of you."

My first impulse was to laugh. I stifled it as Angela put a firm hand on Brooke's shoulder, imploring her to sit back down.

Brooke sat, her thin arms crossed tight over her chest, like a self-imposed straitjacket.

"An item of clothing has gone missing from Brooke's suitcase," Angela explained. "It was brought to my attention this morning, and after conducting a thorough search of Brooke's bedroom and the laundry facilities to no avail, I see no recourse but to bring the issue up in a meeting."

The room went dead. This wasn't a meeting about schedules or allergies or some other minor detail. If I was hearing correctly, Brooke was suggesting that a crime had taken place.

"Brooke?" Angela prompted. "Would you like to walk us through your side of the story?"

I knew I should look straight at Brooke while she delivered

her complaint, but there was a white smear of goat cheese on her left sleeve, and I couldn't tear my eyes away from it.

"Someone went through my personal belongings," she began, her voice quivering with anger. The cheese smear stood out like a bull's eye—why couldn't she eat like a normal person, instead of a pig? If she truly cared about her belongings, why did she cover them in food?

"Someone went through my things while I was asleep," Brooke continued, her nose running. "And they took my favorite dress. My green dress. They stole it from my closet and—" she paused to wipe her nose, which had already dripped into her lap, but launched into another crying jag before she could complete the sentence.

Haley raised her hand. "Are you sure it happened this morning? I mean, what if it happened a few days ago? It could be a mistake—"

"I wore it yesterday," Brooke interjected.

I considered the ramifications of this statement. If she wore it yesterday—and maybe she did, I can't remember—then the dress would have been filthy when she hung it back in her closet. Why would anyone steal a filthy dress? Not to mention an ugly one. It was a vivid green tube-shaped garment that made Brooke look like a Kirby cucumber. If anything, the thief had done her a favor.

After discussing the details of the theft, Angela dispatched us to our rooms to check for missing items of our own. A second item, indeed, was gone.

My leggings.

I have seven pairs of leggings. Seven identical pairs. I wear them every day in summer, firstly because I can't be bothered to wear jeans and secondly because my legs look like tree stumps in shorts. Seven is an easy number to remember—a pair of leggings for each day of the week. As I went through my belongings, I kept counting and recounting, certain that I'd missed a pair. I reported the missing leggings to Angela, who wrote the item down on a list.

How had I gotten implicated in this?

Victoria was spooked. Haley was excited. I, meanwhile, was eager to discuss the details of the robbery with both of them as soon as possible, but I had a session with Alexandra to get through first. This was good in the final analysis, since I had a question I was dying to ask her. I hurried our session along as quickly as possible, impatiently discussing the Caroline business until Alexandra could be persuaded to talk about the theft. Then, as soon as it was possible to do so without being obvious, I asked the question that had been dominating my thoughts for the past hour.

"If the thief were caught," I said, "would she go home?"

"No," Alexandra said, momentarily startled at my introduction of a new topic. She quickly regained her equilibrium, like a surfer navigating a choppy wave. "Absolutely not. It would be something we would work through in group sessions."

"Everyone?"

"Everyone."

"That doesn't seem fair," I said. This was all valuable information, and I needed to extract as much as possible. The Twin Birch memo had covered petty infractions, not serious crimes.

"Why not?"

"Because it's not everyone's fault. To me, it seems like only the thief should be punished."

"And," Alexandra prompted, "you think that the thief should be punished by being sent home?"

Another trick question.

"No, you're right," I said, backtracking. "That wouldn't be a punishment at all."

"Some girls might even view it as a reward," Alexandra said. I could be wrong, but it seemed as though she were watching my reaction with special acuteness. I sensed that I was being tested.

"So no," Alexandra continued, her black bob shining in the sunlight. "We can't go down that disciplinary route. Not for any reason."

"Sounds like a person would have to kill someone to be sent home from Twin Birch," I suggested.

Alexandra raised an eyebrow.

"So what's going to happen?" I asked, redirecting the conversation. "What will happen to the thief when she gets caught?"

"I doubt the thief will get caught," Alexandra said.

"Or confesses?"

"I doubt the thief will confess."

"Why not?" I said.

"She's testing boundaries. If the impulse were rooted in greed, she'd have stolen something of value. If the impulse were based in cruelty, she would have stolen an object of sentimental worth. Instead, she chose an old green dress."

"And a pair of leggings," I added.

Alexandra wrote something down on her notepad. Our time was almost up.

After the session, I sprinted outside to the shaded beech grove where I'd agreed to convene with Victoria and Haley. Both girls were already there; their Group Downtime had begun directly after lunch, while I had been in therapy.

"Nancy Drew to the rescue!" Victoria crowed as I burst out of the front door and ran over to join them. I was breathless with impatience. We immediately began discussing the crime.

"Why clothes?" Victoria speculated. "If you're going to steal, why not steal something of value?"

"Right," I said. "It's not the leggings themselves. I have a million pairs of leggings. Seven, to be exact."

"You're right. It's the weirdness factor," Haley agreed. She tugged on a pair of gold earrings. "I take these off every night. It's not like someone couldn't just grab them from the nightstand. Brooke's dress was, like, fifty years old and stained. It doesn't make sense."

"Clearly, personal gain wasn't the motivation here," I said.

"Then what was?"

We stewed over this question. In doing so, I happened to notice that my thighs had expanded another half-inch or so. I wondered, objectively, how much wider they'd gotten over the past nine days. One inch? Two inches? Three? I wore the same leggings I always wear: black, size XS, opaque enough so that I never have to worry about my underwear showing through. The perfect leggings. For the past few months, I've barely worn anything else.

But that wasn't the subject at hand.

"Do you think this happens a lot?" I asked. "Thefts at Twin Birch?"

"I dunno," Haley said. "Angela seemed weirded out by it."

"Yeah," Victoria agreed. "She wasn't acting on precedent. The meeting was so haphazard—it was like she didn't know what to do. She was improvising."

"She was so serious," I said, giggling a little. "I mean, the action itself is disturbing, but the details of it—the fact that the person stole my leggings . . ."

"It doesn't make sense," Haley agreed. "Unless it was done purely out of malice."

"That's the whole point," Victoria said. "That's why Angela is so concerned."

"Well, following that theory, I can understand why someone would take a disliking to Brooke. She's confrontational and frosty and generally a pill." I snuck a glance at Victoria and Haley to see if they expressed any agreement with my summary, but it was hard to tell. "But me?" I continued. "I'm not exactly a mean person. Why would someone want revenge on me? Why me and Brooke?"

Then I thought of something. The thought must have showed on my face, because Victoria and Haley instantly pounced on it.

"What?" they said simultaneously.

"You have an evil look on your face," Victoria said. She scrambled up to a sitting position and thumped the grass with both hands. "Tell me, tell me, tell me."

"What-what-what!?" Haley said.

"I'm having a Harriet the Spy moment."

"Go on," they begged.

I plucked a stalk of clover and removed the leaves contemplatively, drawing out the gesture for maximum dramatic impact. If I smoked cigarettes, I would've taken the moment to unleash a perfect, languorous line of smoke rings. Oh well.

Victoria poked me in the leg. "What're you plotting?" she asked. "I'm going to die here."

"Don't die yet," I said, with a Cheshire Cat smile. "I know exactly how to catch our thief."

Dear Elise,

Day eleven. We picked raspberries today. Soft, squishy raspberries that we gathered from the brambles and deposited in empty yogurt containers, where the riper ones exploded on impact. I conducted an experiment while I picked, consuming a single berry to see if it tasted any different eaten outside than it did eaten inside. You know what? It did. Standing waist-deep in a patch of thorns and rolling the seeds around on my tongue, I could taste all the other elements that conspired to produce that raspberry: dew, thorns, warmth, and even, not unpleasantly, dirt. I was hypnotized by the taste for three full minutes, and I didn't eat another berry for fear that the taste would go away. The rest of the morning's harvest went directly into my yogurt container. Plop, plop, plop.

Have you ever noticed that a raspberry has a hollow center after you pick it? It's the only berry I can think of that does. Blackberries don't, blueberries don't, and strawberries don't. Why is that? (So elves can wear raspberries as hats?)

In cooking, we simmered and strained the berries to make jam—a process which left everyone's fingers and lips stained a bright Valentine's Day pink. The air smelled like cakes and confections. It reminded me of your very first Valentine.

(Is it significant that I remember *your* first Valentine but not my own? Probably, but I won't attempt to interpret.)

We were in third grade at the time, way too big for printed turtlenecks and kooky socks but not advanced enough for training bras. It was a transitional age. (Then again, what age prior to full-fledged adulthood *isn't* transitional? I can't remember a time when I didn't feel too old or too young.)

We were, at any rate, pre-romantic. Our interests included carnivorous plants, Lip Smackers, T-shirts that changed color in the sun, and squishy pencil grips. We still thought the best way to get boys to like us was to imitate them and/or beat them at HORSE.

What innocent children we were!

February 13 was like Christmas Eve at my house. It was major. Under my mom's watch, V-Day involved treasure hunts, doilies, heart-shaped stickers, unrestrained consumption of glucose, and surprises. Your parents, by contrast, were more or less indifferent to holidays that didn't revolve around the consumption of specialty cocktails (gin and tonics for Independence Day, egg nogs for Christmas, Kir Royals for New Year's—hell, even *I've* committed their drinking schedule to memory by now). Although our parents weren't keen on the idea of sleepovers on school nights, you were always allowed to spend the night on February 13, and this occasion was no different.

The scene outside was brutal when we woke up. A blizzard the week before had left souvenirs of gray ice and filthy slush to crowd the sidewalks, and for weeks the sky had been the color of old clam chowder. Grim weather usually has a leaking effect, wherein it seems to seep indoors and turn everything dull, cold, and dreary. On Valentine's Day, however, the effect was a *contrasting* one. As we traipsed to the kitchen in our matching pajamas like a couple of baby bears, we couldn't believe how snug and warm the little apartment felt. The holiday had transformed a drab apartment into a magical one.

The smell of melting chocolate poured forth from the stove, where my mother was stirring a pot of home-made cocoa. We squealed, and my brother Harry, who was already up and dressed and waiting at the table, tossed us each a red jellybean from the stash he was working through. Red tissue flowers and glitter festooned the table, where giant heart-shaped cookies marked each of our places. ZOE, ELISE, HARRY, and MOM: Our names were spelled out in pink frosting. My mom kissed our foreheads and poured cocoa and flutes of sparkling pear cider for everyone, and we toasted to Valentine's Day. (Harry: "Did you know that toasting was originally a way to make sure that Romans didn't poison each other's drinks? You're supposed to splash a little of your drink into the other person's glass when you clink—that way, if they've tried to poison you, then they'll die too." Mom: "I don't think that's true.") After toasting we feasted on stiff fondant icing and butter cookies, inciting a sugar high that would spin itself out by mid-morning. In two minutes flat, our pajamas were covered in glitter. We were allowed to go to school without brushing our teeth.

It was during math lab that afternoon that Ms. Philpott called you out into the hallway. I figured it was something minor, but when you failed to return after fifteen minutes, I asked permission to use the bathroom and went a-searching for you. The coat closet was vacant, so I checked the hallway and stairwells. Nothing. On a hunch—yep, I'd been reading *Cam Jansen* mysteries—I headed for the girls' bathroom, where my suspicion was speedily confirmed. A flurry of noise came to a halt as I opened the door and slipped inside. Although the bathroom was silent, I detected ragged breathing amid the disinfectant-scented air.

"Elise?" I whispered.

The door to the big handicapped stall inched open.

You stood behind it, looking as though you'd recently killed someone and I'd caught you disposing of the corpse.

"What are you doing?" I cried, rushing inside and locking the stall door behind me. You backed away and slouched unhappily against the wall, your apple-red corduroys still bedazzled in the morning's glitter. A torn pile of fabric stood at your feet, shredded into something that looked like cartoon roadkill. Scraps of fake fur littered the linoleum floor right up to the seat of the toilet, and when I peered inside the bowl, I saw more fluff drifting in the water.

"What on earth—?" I began.

"Ms. Philpott called me outside," you said. "She said that someone had something special for me, and that I should open it."

"Oh God."

"She gave me this bag and watched me open it," you said. "There was a teddy bear inside with a heart on it, and a note from—from—"

"Who?" I asked.

You cringed. "Aaron."

"Oh, *gross.*"

Aaron was the class creep. Not the class *nerd*, but the class *creep*. There's a big difference. The creep is the kid who pushed girls over in kindergarten so he could see their underwear. The kid who would go on to snap their bras a few years later to humiliate them for committing the crime of entering puberty. If cooties were an actual disease, Aaron would have been patient zero. I mean it. He should have been quarantined anyway.

"I am *so* sorry," I said, feeling your pain.

"I think he got his mom to write the note."

"Where is it?" I asked.

"In there." You pointed to the toilet. I looked inside, but the note had dissolved into multicolored mush.

"What'd it say?" I asked.

"Dear Elise, Be my Valentine. Love, Aaron."

"Shut the front door," I gasped. "*Love,* Aaron?"

"Yeah. Ms. Philpott watched me open it. A tablespoon of barf came up in my throat, and I had to swallow it."

I completely understood.

"She told me I had to *thank* him," you went on. "That he'd probably saved up his money to buy it."

"Screw that," I said, stalking over to the toilet. I aimed my sneaker at the handle and kicked, flushing Aaron's icky Valentine into the sewage abyss where it belonged. Then I fixed you up, dipping paper towels in cold water and patting your forehead and cheeks until the color faded from firetruck red to passable pink. We speed-walked back to class, hoping that our absence hadn't drawn attention. I wanted to murder Aaron on your behalf for daring to impose his weirdo desires on you. Mega yuck.

It wasn't the last time I'd experience that particular kind of protective possessiveness. Five or six years later, it began to happen every day. Guys of varying creepiness — and sometimes even *hot* guys — followed you down the supermarket aisle to compliment your eyes. When we went to the bookstore, the guy behind the counter slipped you a note with his phone number. The Apple Store Geniuses fixed your computer for free. It became a source of joking between us.

Aaron's Valentine, however, was the first such milestone in our friendship. Until that moment, I'd never really drawn distinctions between us. We were like matching socks or two Twinkies in a package: a pair, and therefore the same. But from that day forward, we weren't the same anymore.

I paid close attention to this fact.

At the time, I was relieved that I didn't have to dispose of hostile teddy bears on Valentine's Day. But as time passed, the feeling mutated from relief into despair. I saw the way boys looked at you and the way adults talked about you. I began to understand that the glow of beauty that enveloped you was not transferable to me. I felt a gulf widening between us, and although I knew it would always be a part of our friendship, I could never quite accept it.

I wonder if you despise me for admitting these things. It is okay if you do. I thought I would feel better after I wrote them down, but it turns out that I don't. Not really. What I feel instead is ambivalence. I wish that I could gather every last bit of my unhappiness into a ball, just so it would all be in one place.

Love,
Zoe

# [day twelve]

*Too busy plotting* to write more than a few sentences.

One: Today I ate cheesecake for the first time in three years.

Two: We are going to catch the thief.

That is all.

# [Day Thirteen]

*An atmosphere of safety is paramount to the Twin Birch program. For this reason, patients are forbidden from entering each other's personal quarters without explicit, verbal permission.*

*I'd memorized the paragraph carefully.* As in legal documents, seemingly minor details of wording were imbued with the potential to wreak dire consequences.

By now, a curiosity of this notebook should be obvious to anybody who happens to read it (though I don't expect such an event ever to occur): for all of my documentation of Twin Birch, not a *single word* has been written about the other girls' bedrooms. Why not? Read the above paragraph, lifted verbatim from the section of the brochure that I assigned myself to read last night. With the exception of roommates and Devon, nobody is allowed to enter (read: snoop inside) anyone else's bedroom.

The prohibition itself lends extra import to Brooke's accusation, because wrapped up in that crime is included the *additional* crime of trespassing.

Not only is accusing somebody of theft a big deal, as Brooke had publicly accused me, Haley, and Victoria, but investigating the crime ourselves by, say, sneaking around to see if our belongings show up in somebody else's suitcase is a logistical impossibility. Our whereabouts are always accounted for, even during Group Downtime. There are no opportunities to prowl.

Except, of course, at night. How else do you think I've been reading the all-important memo?

For the past four days, a scheme had been brewing in my mind. I had to be careful and meticulous in the planning. I couldn't afford to mess up on this.

I mentioned the plan to Victoria and Haley yesterday but told them I needed twenty-four more hours in order to work out the details. They pleaded with me for ten minutes but ultimately agreed to the caveat, and I promised them that it would be worth it.

"Trust me," I told them at last night's dinner. "I need to sleep on it and work out the kinks. I'll tell you tomorrow over breakfast."

In truth, I didn't need twenty-four hours. Or anything close to it. What I needed was ten minutes of uninterrupted reading time in the bathroom—but I could only accomplish this task at night, after everyone else was asleep. I was fairly certain that my memory was correct—that there was a loophole in the Twin Birch rules that we could exploit for our own purposes—but I needed to pore over the brochure one last time, checking the fine print and rereading the rules to ensure that I had them fully memorized.

Plus, I was nervous. I hadn't asserted myself much at Twin Birch, and this would be asserting myself big-time. The longer I could put it off, the more time I had to get over my fears.

It wasn't difficult to find an interval in which to sneak to the bathroom at lights-out, since I was wired enough to know that I wouldn't be getting much sleep. Caroline was a minor problem; it took her a full hour to fall asleep, and I waited an additional hour for certainty's sake, given that my ability to read her sleep patterns had been proven faulty on the night that she launched her surprise-attack interrogation. At half-past midnight, I slinked out of bed, locked myself in the bathroom, found what I needed to know, and proceeded to imprint the wording on my brain by a monotonous process of rote rereading.

Breakfast the next morning was a rainbow chard omelet with romesco sauce. Nobody had a clue what romesco sauce was, which gave Devon—who sat at the other table—ample opportunity to speechify on the subject while Victoria, Haley, and I got down to brass tacks.

"Here's the idea," I whispered, propping my elbows on the table. "We each have a roommate. Technically, searching our roommate's stuff is against the rules, but it's not a rule that's strictly enforceable by anyone except your roommate. Got it?"

They nodded.

"Then you grind the almonds into a paste, so it's like glue," Devon was loudly explaining at the other table. The three of us reflexively looked down at the orangey-red sauce covering our omelets. There were *nuts* in this? Great.

"Anyway," I went on. "Imaginary scenario: Let's say Devon walks by your bedroom and catches you pawing through a suitcase. She's gonna assume it's your suitcase, not your roommate's. Therefore, we can all search our roommate's suitcases to make sure that the dress isn't in there."

"And your leggings," Haley added.

"And my leggings. Exactly."

"Hold on," Victoria said. "Me and Haley are roommates."

"Right. This is about process of elimination. *I* know you guys didn't steal the stuff, but for thoroughness's sake, do a search through each other's suitcases. Just to be sure. I'll search Caroline's stuff when she's out of the room."

Victoria and Haley looked at each other, screwing up their noses. "That's so weird!" Haley said. "Isn't that awkward?"

"Not unless you have something to hide," I said deviously.

"Oh my God, you're like a trial lawyer," Victoria said. "Okay, I'm game. Haley and I can search each other as soon as Gardening is over."

"Perfect. I'll do Caroline when she's in therapy. We can report our results during lunch."

"Wait," Victoria said. "What about you?"

"What about what?"

"Your stuff. If we ask Caroline to search your suitcase, she's gonna run straight to Devon and tattle on us. We can't tell her."

I rolled my eyes. "Why would I steal my own leggings?" I asked.

Haley and Victoria were silent for a moment. I tensed. Was it silly of me to think that they would take my innocence for granted?

But Victoria nodded at last. "You're right," she said.

Devon's blaring voice carried over from the next table. "Then, when the bread is toasted," she was saying, "you add it to the food processor with oil, vinegar, peppers, and the nuts from earlier." Her enthusiasm was going over like a lead balloon—Caroline drew swirls in her romesco sauce, and Jane stared at the floor. Incredible. Sometimes I liked to observe Devon strictly for the spectacle of her unbreakable self-confidence.

"Thoroughness is essential," I said, breaking my gaze from the bobbing blond ponytail to return to our strategy session. "Let's meet on the lawn as soon as warm-up is finished. If all goes well, we can cross four names off our list."

"Genius," Victoria said. "And so simple, too."

"Yep, process of elimination," I shrugged. "Just think of it like a standardized test."

Boogers.

That was the word that came to mind as Devon shoveled ricotta gnocchi on my plate. *Giant boogers*. Garden tomatoes, balsamic onions, and a confetti of pine nuts went on top of the gnocchi, which I carried back to my table like a prisoner dragging a ball and chain. At least I could find my way to the dining room on my own now.

It was lunchtime and Victoria and Haley awaited me, their plates already loaded and steaming. We were all eager to share our results.

"So," I said, sitting down. "You two first."

Haley pointed at Victoria. "All clear," she said.

"Ditto," Victoria replied.

"No dirty green dress? No leggings that smell like gazpacho?" (I'd spilled Devon's disgusting gazpacho on my leggings the other day.)

They both shook their heads.

"Me neither," I said. "There was nothing in Caroline's suitcase but St. Agnes paraphernalia and Kate Spade headbands."

"Huh," Victoria said under her breath. "To be honest, I was kind of suspecting Caroline. There's something maladjusted about her."

"Agreed."

"Well, what do we do now?" Haley asked, chasing a piece of gnocchi around her plate. "Our ploy didn't work."

"Hold your horses," I said. "That was only half of the plan."

"It was?"

We were interrupted by an enthusiastic noise at the other table. Devon was smacking herself on the forehead.

"KALE CHIPS!" Devon yelped. "I forgot the *kale* chips!" We watched her shoot up and run into the kitchen, returning with two baskets that contained the results of our earlier kitchen labor.

"Fabulous—more food," Victoria muttered. "I was hoping she forgot."

Each table got its own basket of kale chips. "You guys, I am so sorry," Devon said.

She returned to the other table, her ponytail animated in flight.

"As I was saying," I continued. "We know for sure that none of us is the perp."

"You did *not* just say 'perp,'" Victoria said.

"I totally did. So listen, here's what we do. When dinner rolls around, the three of us huddle together conspiratorially and talk in whispers. Why? Because we want Jane and Brooke to see us scheming. After all, we know that one of them is the thief—"

"But it was Brooke's dress," Haley interrupted.

"Please," I rejoined. "Brooke is nuts. She easily could have stolen her own dress to get sympathy points. And if she was going to steal anyone else's clothes along with it, she'd choose mine because she loathes me. So," I went on. "Immediately following dinner, during warm-up, we three all stand up at my signal in the living room, and we make a little announcement."

"A little announcement," Victoria echoed.

"Correct. We say, 'Listen up, ladies. We know what's up. We know what's missing and we also know who took it.'"

"But we don't," Haley pointed out.

"Doesn't matter. It's a bluff," Victoria said, nodding. She was starting to understand what I was getting at.

"Oh," said Haley.

"Right," I continued. "We stand up in front of everyone and say some version of the following: The thief knows who she is. And so do we. Frankly, we'd like nothing more than to rat her out and see her gone from this place. But lucky for her, we have an ounce of empathy in our hearts. Therefore, we're willing to strike a compromise. If we see the clothes returned to their proper places by bedtime tonight, we'll consider the case closed. Finished. Understood?"

"That's good," Victoria said. "That's genius."

"I have goose bumps." Haley shivered. "Do you think it will really work?"

"Haven't you ever played poker?" I speared a gnocchi and held it up to the light. Haley reached into the basket of kale chips, selected the tiniest one, and put it in her mouth, wincing slightly. "What matters most," I said, "is delivery. Without an impeccable delivery, this plan will fail. Like all bluffs."

"This is actually good," Haley said, crunching on her chip. "Eat one. I promise it's good."

I ate a kale chip. It was good. Salty and crunchy and vaguely satisfying. "This is the first thing we've made that I like," I acknowledged.

"It tastes frizzly," Haley said.

"Not a word," Victoria mumbled, clearly not interested in proving Haley right.

"I know, but eat one. You'll see what I mean."

Victoria took a kale chip. "Huh," she said. "I see what you mean." She finished chewing and then held up a finger. "I hate to be a killjoy, Zoe, but there's a glaring flaw in this plan."

*Crap.* What had I forgotten?

"The flaw is this," Victoria went on. "If we play this right, you'll get your leggings back, but we still won't know who took them in the first place. We still won't know who we can and can't trust."

She was right. I'd recognized the flaw from the plan's inception; I was just hoping no one else would notice.

I nibbled at a kale chip while I pretended to mull over her objection. "You're right," I said. "But it still seems like a small price to pay. The main thing is that it will curb any future thefts. If the person knows that she's been caught or thinks that she's been caught, she's not going to risk doing it again. That would be suicide."

"True," Victoria said. "Okay. You've convinced me. I'm on board."

"Me too," Haley said. "This is fun. This is like a *CSI* episode."

"Excellent," I confirmed. As with any solid plan, the execution was a basic matter of rehearsing and carrying out the motions. Having settled on a course of action, we picked up our forks and started fiddling with the gnocchi, which were now cold and slimy (for extra booger-verisimilitude).

Somehow, the basket of kale chips had emptied out during the conversation without our even noticing it.

*That*, I thought cynically, *was a first.*

**Crispy Kale Chips for Sleuths**
1 bunch of kale
3 tbsp. olive or coconut oil
3 cloves garlic, minced
Pinch of salt

Preheat oven to 500 degrees. Tear kale into pieces about half the size of your fist. (Don't sweat the technique—the size of the pieces doesn't much matter.) In a big bowl, pour other ingredients on top. Squeeze, knead, and/or massage the whole thing with your hands until the kale is soft (about one minute). Spread on a baking sheet and cook six minutes in the oven, stirring once or twice. If the kale isn't crispy after six minutes, keep cooking. Just don't let your leaves burn!

Recipe produces a large batch, best shared with co-conspirators.

Having paved the road with Haley and Victoria for the rest of the day, I decided to strike out on my own for a pre-dinner walk around the grounds. The adrenaline stoked by our plan mingled with that peculiar heightened feeling that summer nights can have, and it seemed to me that the grass smelled grassier than usual. The feeling was anticipatory, like creeping downstairs to open your Christmas stocking or getting an e-mail that you've been tagged on Facebook. Except that this time, there was an added tinge of fear. After two laps around the shambling brick building—Twin Birch's isolation means that we're allowed to roam unsupervised, since there's no possible route of escape—I found a thick spot on the lawn and lay down, staring upward. The tree leaves waved like tiny silk fans. I reached for my phone to take a picture and then stopped, remembering where I was. My phone was locked away.

Perhaps it is a predictable observation, but being without a cellphone makes me aware of how infrequently I actually have the chance to indulge in long thoughts without the possibility of interruption. I hadn't noticed before, but every time a text popped up on my phone (or on Elise's), it created a tiny, near-invisible distraction. And while tiny distractions are not in themselves harmful, they do add up into an implacable distance, and a distance that you eventually stop noticing because it so quickly becomes the norm. As I lay flat on my back, letting the breeze tickle my nose, I began to wonder how deep a conversation between two people can be if you're both aware that you may be interrupted at a moment's notice.

Maybe it makes no difference.

At quarter to seven I got up to wash my hands and prepare for dinner. Haley and Victoria were lingering by the door when I arrived at the dining room, waiting for Devon to choose her seat so that we could sit at the other table. Very strategic.

"It smells like a fart in here," Haley observed.

"Roasted broccoli," Victoria said. "A wild guess."

She was right. Roasted broccoli, corn chowder with smoked cheddar, and sprouted flax bread. Dessert was a blackberry-fig cobbler that nobody but Devon partook of. If it is hard enough to choke down our meals on an ordinary day, today was even worse. There's nothing like pre-performance jitters to flush your appetite down the toilet.

Although I was careful not to act unusual, I did make one small mistake while Devon was in the kitchen fetching dessert. I allowed my eyes to wander over to Caroline, Jane, and Brooke—in retrospect, I wonder if a sixth sense guided me to do so—and caught them bent forward at their table, taking advantage of Devon's absence to whisper an urgent exchange. When Brooke caught my eye, she clamped her mouth shut and reeled back into her chair with a look of alarm, as though I'd been reading her lips.

If only.

Figs and blackberries were followed by herbal tea and warm-up period. The possibility of a movie was introduced. At that point, the mission unfolded exactly as I'd hoped.

On my signal, we stood up, shed our blankets, gathered at the front of the living room, and faced the group.

"What's up, girls?" Devon asked, startled.

We didn't reply. Instead, we delivered our announcement, as choreographed, with confidence and simplicity. As a postscript, I added the following:

"Victoria, Haley, and I will spend the next forty minutes outside on the lawn, star-gazing, in order to provide the thief enough time to return the garments to their original places without fear of being caught. All that matters," I said, "is that the items are returned. That's all. We have no interest in punishment, entrapment, or deception."

Devon's eyes bugged like a goldfish's, but she was frozen, too stunned at our audacity to commandeer the situation. And why should she? Our plan was a good one. It was a fair and decent one. After concluding our statement, we filed out the door, down the stairs, and out to the lawn. The evening air was translucent; our bodies shook with excitement.

"That went well, right?" Haley blurted, as soon as we were a safe distance from the house.

"It did," I said cautiously. "But we can't celebrate yet."

Victoria was quiet.

"What's up?" I nudged her. We lay down on our stomachs, slapping away mosquitos.

"Nothin'," she said unconvincingly. "That was good."

"Spill," I said. "You're worried about something."

Victoria rolled over onto her back. "I am," she admitted. "It's the fact that even if the plan works, we still won't know who committed the crime. I know that we don't have any other options, but it still bugs me. I'm still creeped out."

I frowned in the dark. Her comment annoyed me. *She* hadn't offered a better plan, had she? I'd stayed up *hours* in order to read the damn Twin Birch memo and iron out the intricacies of our action, and she wasn't satisfied? God.

Victoria seemed to read my thoughts because she hurriedly amended her opinion. "Scratch that. Zoe, I'm being retarded."

"I just don't know what the alternative is."

"I know. We're taking the high-minded approach, and I'm being a baby about it. Forget it. Don't listen to me."

"I *do* see what you mean, though," I said, feeling generous after she'd admitted being wrong.

"No, you're right about it," Victoria added. "It's not about making someone feel bad. It's about fixing a weird situation so we can bury it in the past and not let it bother us. Your plan is good. It's really good."

"Hear, hear," Haley agreed.

*Whew.*

"It is going to be torture staying out here for forty minutes," Haley said. "Like, I want to run inside right now and see if your leggings are back in their drawer," she said.

"You're telling me," Victoria replied. "I'm the one with ADD."

"You are?" I asked.

"Well, I assume so. Self-diagnosed."

We cracked up.

"My hair is ADD, too," Victoria added.

When forty minutes were up, we sprang to our feet and headed quietly toward the house. A sense of calm had overtaken me, but Victoria and Haley were practically skipping with eagerness to check on the results of our experiment. Ever so softly, we opened the entrance door and climbed up the main steps. Since we couldn't enter Brooke's room, our beeline was directed toward mine. If my leggings were back in their original spot, then presumably Brooke's dress would be back in her closet.

I opened the door to my bedroom. Caroline sat upright on the bed, a book of crossword puzzles balanced on her knees. I stopped short, causing Haley and Victoria to bump up against me. I hadn't expected my roommate to be a witness to our mission.

"Hey," I said, smiling in an effort to conceal my surprise.

Caroline looked up but said nothing and quickly returned to her crossword puzzle. The boldness she'd shown on the night she pummeled me with questions (*Why are you here?*) was nowhere in evidence. Perhaps the presence of Victoria and Haley intimidated her. It hardly mattered.

I walked to the chest of drawers, pulled out the uppermost drawer, and extracted my neatly folded stack of leggings. Together, the three of us counted: one . . . two . . . three . . . four . . . five.

"*Five?*" Haley shrieked. "The thief took another pair!"

"No, they didn't, nerd," Victoria corrected her. "She's wearing one of the pairs."

"Oh," Haley blushed, eyeing the leggings I had on. "My bad."

Victoria chewed her lip. "Dammit," she said.

"Dammit to hell," Haley said. "What do we do now? I'm pissed."

"Me too," Victoria said. "And I have to pee. No pun intended."

She left the room, leaving Haley and I standing dumbfounded with a rumpled quintet of leggings. "We need to think this through," I started to say. "We need—"

"ZOE!"

A scream punctured the air. Caroline looked up, terrified, as Victoria skidded into the room. In her hands were a green rag and a ball of black fabric.

"In the bathroom!" she shrieked. "Brooke's dress—your leggings—they were piled up next to the sink—"

She dropped the leggings in my hands and held the dress out to examine it. Dribbles and splotches of God knows what covered the front of the garment. It was definitely Brooke's dress.

"It makes sense," Victoria said breathlessly, brandishing the garments to underline her point. "The culprit must have been afraid that someone would see her entering our rooms, so she stashed it in the bathroom for us to find." She boinked herself on the head with the back of her hand. "Duh! We should have thought of that!"

Now *she* was right.

Amid the excitement, we were aware of an uncomfortable presence in the room. Gaping at us with her jaw slack, Caroline bore stony witness to the celebration.

"I don't understand," Caroline said slowly. "You said you knew who did it."

"We bluffed," Haley said proudly. "And lookie here? We found the goods!"

"But you *tricked* us."

"Why does it matter?" Victoria said impatiently. "Who cares? Aren't you happy that Brooke got her dress back?"

"I don't think it's right to trick anyone," Caroline pushed back.

"I can't believe we're having this conversation," Victoria said, getting steamed. "Are you honestly telling me that you'd prefer we didn't recover the clothes?"

Caroline stared back at Victoria with placid eyes, then turned back to her book and filled out a crossword answer. It was an infuriating display of glibness.

"You're just smug," Victoria continued, "because none of your things got stolen. If we hadn't done what we just did, your precious little picture frames might just be the next thing to go. How would you feel then? Would you still be a smirking little—"

"*WHAT* is going on here?" Devon thundered, breaking up the argument.

*Here we go,* I thought.

Victoria took a deep breath and turned to face Devon. "Zoe's plan worked," she explained. "Look. We got Brooke's dress back. And Zoe's leggings. The thief left everything in the bathroom for us to find."

Devon stared at the two items, her mouth set in a grim line. For the second time that week, she seemed genuinely confused. The air was thick with ambiguity. For a split second, nobody knew what to do.

The moment didn't last long. Something clicked back into place, and Devon ordered us to bed in a clipped, militaristic tone.

"I need to brush my teeth," Haley said.

"All of you in bed. Now."

"But—" Haley protested.

"I said *now*." Devon glared as Haley and Victoria wheeled out of my room, giving me silent thumbs-up signs on their way out. Devon, her hands folded against her chest, remained. Was she going to punish me? Praise me? I had no clue. Her expression was befuddling—or maybe just befuddled.

"We'll discuss this in the morning," she said at last.

I understood why she was upset. Her authority had just been toppled, and there was nothing she could do about it. I even felt a little sorry for Devon. But by the time I could answer or explain myself, she'd left the room, leaving me alone to change into my PJs and go to sleep.

I pulled a clean T-shirt from my drawer and threw it on, then pulled the coverlet back from my bed and got in. Caroline's side of the room was dark. She lay wrapped in her blanket, facing the wall and breathing unevenly.

We lay there, awake, in the dark.

Dear Elise,

Where are you? Why aren't you responding?

I'm sorry. Ignore that. Pleading and blaming is no way to start a letter. It hasn't even been that long since I wrote, I guess. Did my first few letters get lost in the mail? Either option is more probable than the circumstance of you ignoring me. I know you'd never do that.

Have you left town unexpectedly? That's probably it. Your mom must be collecting my envelopes as they slide through the mailbox. I imagine her stacking them in a bundle on your bed along with issues of *Vogue* and *Teen Vogue* and *Vogue UK*. Just thinking of those glossy, perfumed magazines—banned at Twin Birch, of course—makes me itch with displeasure at the stuff I'm missing out on. If I were in the city with you, we'd be sitting in the shade outside with a whole afternoon's worth of magazines, sipping Pellegrino from the bottle. Your mom would poke her head out, yell at us for drinking from the bottle, and extort promises to use glasses next time, which we would never do. Pellegrino tastes infinitely better from the bottle.

There are other reasons why you might not be responding to me, I suppose. Less innocent reasons.

Your mom might be intercepting the letters. This thought has occurred to me. She might even be reading them.

I hope not.

I think you've probably left town for some reason. That's the most likely explanation.

Things have calmed down here, at least relative to the seismic upheaval of the past few days. Devon managed to extinguish her anger, and after breakfast this morning, she even propped open the windows in the living room so we could watch the idyllic summer scene unfold beyond. Morning doves cooed, dragonflies swooped, lilies grew sunward. Some people would consider it paradise.

I, on the other hand, could think of nothing beyond the now-predictable turmoil in my stomach. It was a heavy, damp feeling, as though I'd swallowed a bucket of minnows. I could feel them swimming in a pit of water, sloshing back and forth. I held myself with both hands, cringing and willing myself not to think about what I'd just ingested. It was much easier to shovel in food when

I was in denial about how long I'd be sentenced to Twin Birch. *It won't take long to undo the damage,* I kept telling myself. But how long will it take to undo thirty-six days of damage? And what if I can't undo it?

Being force-fed is more than a physical experience— it's also an emotional one. Take a moment to think about it. When was the last time somebody forced you to eat? I don't mean your parents hectoring you about that last piece of breaded fish left on your plate, or the soggy broccoli abandoned in the steamer. I mean *truly* forced to eat, and forced to eat food that you never wanted in the first place.

If you can't remember the last time it happened, there's a very good reason for that: It doesn't happen much. It's not natural for people our age to be forced into any biological activity. As a result, the process of being obliged to eat makes me—and everyone else here, I think—feel infantile. When I come home, I'll look even younger than I usually do. My baby cheeks will be plumper; my fingers will be like breakfast sausages rather than matchsticks.

Don't be revolted when you see me. The waistband of my leggings—which I wear specifically *because* they make it impossible to tell how fat or thin I am at any given moment—pinches deeper each day, leaving a circumference of red skin when I strip them off at night. Throughout this letter I've been taking breaks to put the pen down and trace the painful marks around my waist with a fingertip. I check them every thirty seconds to see if the swelling has decreased, but I can't really tell the difference.

Still, I feel different tonight than I did yesterday. Less angry. If I were to paint myself on a canvas, I'd choose a different color—perhaps a pale blue?—today, whereas the past week has been composed of angry crimson slashes. Blue is better than red, though I do feel as though I am *literally* depressed. As though someone has dug a hole in the ground and laid me down inside of it.

I really miss you.

During Group Downtime today, I went to my bedroom while Haley and Victoria hung out. I took off my shoes, sat cross-legged on the bed, and closed my eyes. Then I did something I've never done before: I meditated.

Or maybe it was the opposite of meditation. I don't know. What I did was to focus all of my neurons on a single task. The task was to comb through the past and think about every food-related memory that I could find. And then, once I'd located the memories, to find within them all of the parts that proved my normalcy. By doing so, I reasoned, I could begin to solve the problem at hand: I could convince Alexandra that I do not have an eating disorder, contrary to my mother's conviction, and that I should not be surrounded by girls who do.

I could go home in time to spend the rest of the summer with you.

After perching in swami position for fifteen minutes,

I had a handful of memories in mind. I reached down beneath the bed and plucked a notecard from my box of supplies, then started composing a list. I saw, as I wrote, that my memories of food overlapped extensively with my memories of you. The overlap was almost complete.

The list is not finished yet.

Why haven't you written back?


Love,
Zoe

# [Day sixteen]

**Breakfast:**
Blended beet, carrot, and orange juice (8 oz.)
Cornmeal pancakes with butter and blueberry jam
Honeydew melon

**Lunch:**
Roast tomato and garlic soup
Zucchini fritters
Whole-grain toast (2 slices)

**Dinner:**
Moroccan vegetable stew
Hummus (1/4 c)
Pita bread (2 slices)
Coconut chai pudding (*didn't eat)

Dear Elise,

Am I writing too much? Probably. I need to distract myself from two things: the food I am eating and—ironically—the fact that you're not writing back. Composing a letter to you solves neither problem, but at least it provides a distraction. At least it keeps me from having bad thoughts.

It's day seventeen and I'm thinking about you non-stop. I'm not mad about my letters going unanswered, I promise. Not even an ounce of mad. Just nervous.

Food is the other thing. By now I've gained at least five pounds. My flesh bulges and my gait is heavier. I can't bear to look at myself in the mirror—not even my face, which is the only thing that's visible, anyhow. In this entire castle of a house, there's not a single full-length mirror. The omission is not an accident.

I can pinch part of my thigh between my fingers to form a roll. How does a person gain weight so quickly? It's mathematical. Calories in, calories out. By ten a.m. here I've eaten more than I would normally eat in three days. Can you imagine? I keep notes on the food like the other girls, and I tally up calories. Black bean burgers, cilantro guacamole, peach crisp with lemon-pistachio topping, chewy pumpkin squares. Faux-healthy food. It all makes me gag.

My friend Victoria imposes a mental grid over her food and proceeds to cut it into tiny cubes, which she eats one at a time. She says it helps her swallow.

Another girl, Brooke—decidedly *not* a friend—has to sit next to Devon at every meal because she has adopted a strategy of swallowing her food whole, without chewing it, and one day she almost choked. Apparently her theory is that the body can't digest unchewed food, and that therefore food, if swallowed without chewing, can pass through the body without contributing any calories. (This is false. Obviously. And disgusting.)

On some afternoons, I do nothing but digest. I sit on a couch or flat on the grass, wondering *where*, in a physical sense, all the food is going. Don't they say that your stomach is approximately the size of a clenched fist? Well, what happens when a person is forced to eat four times that amount? How much can the stomach handle before it bursts? Or stretches out permanently, like a pair of old pantyhose?

The lightest bread crumb feels heavier than osmium when I pick it up with my fork, and when I swallow, an unstoppable slide show of images comes to mind. As the food finds its way into my stomach, inch by inch, I think of rotten meat and sagging udders and bruised fruit. Heavy, leaking things. I think that's what my stomach probably looks like on the inside, and it makes me feel like puking.

Last month I was light as a feather. Three weeks ago, even.

I remember when you and I first noticed it. I was never fat to begin with, and you were even less so. But at the same time, we didn't look the way we wanted to. My upper arms jiggled. You didn't like the way your thighs looked in skinny jeans. A drastic change was in order, we agreed, and with your laptop in hand, we went out to your front stoop (when was that? A Saturday? In May?) and opened a Google Doc. *Zoe and Elise,* I titled it. That was the beginning. That was when we planned our new regime:

**Breakfast**:
Banana and ½ energy bar

**Lunch**:
Coffee yogurt and one apple

**Snack**:
One apple and unlimited carrot or red pepper sticks

**Dinner**:
As little as possible

**Dessert**:
Light ice cream (1 cup)
or
Candy bar

Dinner, we agreed, was the only potential problem. We often ate with our families, and therefore had no control over what was served. This, however, didn't prove to be difficult: I ate a few spoonfuls here, a few spoonfuls there, fed a few bites to my dog, and shifted everything around on our plates until it looked convincingly worked-over. Nobody noticed a thing—at least, not then. The **Dessert** category was the most fun, and dangerous, to plan, since it required improvisation:

"We need a reward system," I said, as we shared the laptop that day.

"Smart idea," you said, taking the keyboard from me. "A reward is essential. If we're good all day and stick to the plan, we get a treat of our choice. Like puppy training."

"But we can't have anything," I said. "There has to be limits."

"The good ice cream can be one of them," you suggested. The "good ice cream" was a fluffy vanilla confection that came out to 100 calories per serving, although a single serving was too small to satisfy anyone above toddler age. We decided that two servings of good ice cream or a normal-sized candy bar were suitable options for the **Dessert** category, both coming in at about 230 calories. The diet, I stipulated, could be revised as time went on; the important thing was that we adhere to it faithfully. Each day that we successfully stuck to the routine, we'd put a tally mark in the Google Doc. My competitive urges would guarantee that I almost *never* broke the diet. Not that I was competitive with *you*, Elise. Not really, anyway. It's just that when I start a plan, I stick to it.

We celebrated our new plan by measuring out two servings of vanilla ice cream apiece. I remember the look of concentration on your face as you pushed the measuring cup into the carton and leveled it off to exactly 200 calories worth. (In that way, I suppose, you remind me of some of the girls I've met here.) Then we washed the cup, dried it, and returned it to the cupboard. If your parents saw that we'd been measuring our food, they might have gotten suspicious. There was no need to ignite suspicion yet.

The first week was shockingly easy. We were on an adrenaline rush, thrilled with our newfound discipline and bursting with encouragement for each other. "I can already tell the difference," you marveled, after six or seven days. It was late June, not more than a few weeks after our middle school graduation, and we lay sprawled across your bed under the cooling blast of the air conditioner. The laptop was propped between us; we browsed eBay for sundresses without needing or planning to buy anything. It was edging close to dinnertime when you flipped over on your back and asked, with a goofy smile, whether I ever felt high from not eating.

"High? I wish," I said. "No. I just feel like I might become pickled from overconsumption of Splenda. Like if I died unexpectedly my corpse would be perfectly embalmed in Splenda crystals."

"Gross."

"Just being candid."

We had followed our plan to the letter that day, washing down thinly sliced apples and tiny spoonfuls of coffee yogurt with a sea of Fresca, which we poured into the frosty glasses that your parents kept in the freezer for their cocktails. My glass stood on your nightstand, and I drained the last warm drops of soda as I tried to figure out whether my failure to feel high from not eating was something to worry about. "Do *you* feel high?" I asked.

"Yeah. I feel like I just got laughing gas or something," you said. "Float-y. Fun."

You spun a curlicue of white-blond hair around one finger, unswirled it, spun it again, and then laughed.

"Should I be worried? Do you need a frozen grape or something?" I asked. "Half an apple? Fresca?"

"No, I actually like the feeling. It's weird, like being drunk. Or not drunk, but the perfect amount of tipsy." You forked your legs in the air like a starfish. "Feels blissful," you murmured.

I was slightly envious—it was one more thing that came easy to you, one more thing that was better for you than for me. But I trusted you. I still trust you, Elise, although my trust is waning with every day that passes without a letter from you. It's been more than two weeks—where are you? You're never away from the city for this long. And the statistical probability of *all* my letters getting lost in the mail is unfathomable. I don't understand why you're silent when I need you the most.

Write back, please. I need it badly. That's the moral of this story. Write me from wherever you are. It doesn't have to be a long letter; it can be a postcard or any stupid little thing. A single line on a piece of notebook paper. An empty envelope. I don't like being here, and I *really* don't like being here without you.

It's past midnight, now. I'm technically on my eighteenth day. Exactly halfway through.

When I told Alexandra that I was having trouble sleeping, she suggested that I use the time to write a list of memories about you. "How many?" I asked her.

"Twenty," she said.

"Too much," I said, shaking my head.

"How about fifteen?"

I shook my head again.

"Let's aim for fifteen," Alexandra said.

I wasn't intending to capitulate to her advice, but lo and behold, I can't sleep tonight, and I have a hunch that the repetitive motion of writing might act as a sedative. So, here are fifteen memories, in chronological order:

1. I remember meeting you on the first day of kindergarten.

2. I remember that our class turtle smelled like mothballs.

3. I remember how you nominated to name him Cheez-It, and I seconded the nomination.

4. I remember giving each other head lice in second grade.

5. I remember when you asked our third-grade art teacher when neon was invented and how crestfallen you were when she didn't know the answer.

6. I remember researching our favorite topics when we were finally allowed to use the Internet unsupervised: Easter Island, the Bermuda Triangle, leper colonies, phosphorescent jellyfish, Amelia Earhart's disappearance, cults, the Northern Lights.

7. I remember matching pajamas in sixth grade, printed with slices of flying pizza.

8. I remember mispronouncing "epitome."

9. I remember requesting pancakes doughy (a.k.a. raw in the middle) from your dad, then pouring maple syrup on top and mixing it in with the wet dough and eating the whole shebang with a spoon.

10. I remember how the pressure (and our inevitable failure) to do something socially epic on New Year's Eve made us feel thrilled and sad and hurt all at once.

11. I remember being embarrassed about absolutely everything.

12. I remember when guys started checking you out.

13. I remember—though I would never have admitted it—feeling lost in the shadows sometimes when I was with you.

14. I remember wondering whether it was possible for best friends to be soul mates.

15. I remember deciding on the answer.

I remember much more, too. Write me back when you can.

Love,
Zoe

# [day eighteen]

*There was no reason* to think that I'd end the day by blacking out. Then again, I suppose there never is.

We talked about the theft again during my Alexandra session. Specifically, the thief's decision to return the items, and the fact that the perpetrator had stashed the returned items in the bathroom rather than in their proper places. Alexandra asked me why I thought she—the thief—had done this.

"It's obvious," I said. "The thief was embarrassed. She didn't want to be caught. I'm kicking myself that I didn't think of that when we made the announcement."

"You're sensitive about that emotion," Alexandra observed.

"What emotion?"

"Embarrassment. Humiliation."

"Isn't everyone?" I asked. "It's the worst. It's the only emotion that's *physically painful*. My cheeks burn when I blush. Literally. They burn."

The day was unseasonably cold, and I tugged at the fringe of the afghan in my lap. It was so damn fuzzy. What kind of animal did it come from? I wanted one as a pet.

"I want to get to a point in my life," I told Alexandra, "where I'm not constantly being humiliated. Does that ever happen?"

"It does," Alexandra said, "but not for the reasons you think."

"Why then?"

"You never stop doing idiotic things because that's part of being human. That's probably the most fundamental part of being a human. Most of the time, however, we can't see the idiotic things for what they are."

"Which is what?"

"Idiotic," Alexandra said, a slight smile curling her lip. "Being human is funny and bizarre. We do strange things. Most of the time no one else notices. Luckily."

I thought about this.

"For example, we put things into a hole at the top of our body and then, later, those same things come out a different hole at the bottom of our body."

"Eww," I said. "When you put it like that . . ."

"We sit in front of glowing boxes," she continued, "for hours at a time. We cover ourselves in pieces of brightly colored fabric. We have sex. If you think objectively about sex—"

I started laughing against my will.

"Exactly my point," Alexandra said. "If you think objectively about sex, it's the most idiotic thing of all. People working them-selves into different shapes, grunting and sweating and—"

"I get it."

"Good. You see what I mean," Alexandra said. "We're des-tined to look foolish and make mistakes. We grow old and end up looking like wrinkly babies. Our mistakes don't have to be failures."

*Our mistakes don't have to be failures,* I repeated mentally.

"The next time you do something that feels embarrassing, try stepping outside of yourself and having empathy. Say, 'There you go again, Zoe, adding another blooper to the endless blooper reel of life.'"

"The blooper reel of life. I like that."

"What do you think would happen if you did it?"

"If I said those things to myself?" I said. "About the blooper reel? I guess it might help me lighten up."

"A decade ago I taught at a university," Alexandra said. "In upstate New York. A serene, leafy, liberal arts college. The cafete-ria was your typical college eatery: pizza, pasta, a salad bar with mushrooms that tasted like rubber flip-flops."

"I've had those mushrooms," I said. "They taste like ear wax."

"I never thought of it that way. Anyhow, the cafeteria had one stellar feature. There was a water dispenser near the burger sta-tion—just your average tap water-dispensing spigot, and a stack of plastic cups next to it. The water pressure in the dispenser was somehow off. Every time you tried to fill a cup with water, a jet-stream of water would shoot out."

"Jesus," I said.

"Bottom line, everyone who drank water—which was every-one—wound up getting splashed with water at the fountain. Totally soaked. The guys at the burger station didn't even look up when they handed over the wad of napkins for you to clean yourself up with. It must have happened a thousand times a day."

"Why didn't anyone fix it?" I asked.

"Good question. Every single day, I got water all over my blouse. Often in front of my own students, which was humiliating."

I wondered if Alexandra had worn white silk tunics back then, too. A wet, white blouse would be a difficult look to carry off as a professor.

"Every day I promised myself I'd ask the manager to fix the water pressure. But I never did."

I gave her a quizzical look.

"Because," Alexandra continued, "when it came down to it, I admired that stupid fountain. It functioned as a symbol that ulti-mately seemed necessary, despite how annoying it was."

"Confused," I said.

"College is all about hierarchy. At the bottom are the under-graduates. Then come the graduate students. Then the assistant professors, the full professors, and so forth until you get to the very top, which is the president. This water fountain, unlike everything else on campus, saw no difference between an under-graduate and a full professor. It was a machine, so it was neu-tral. And it splashed everyone, regardless of status. No one was spared."

"Huh," I said.

"I came to see it as the great equalizer on campus." She

smiled. "It made everyone a lot nicer, too. You can't exactly be an asshole if you've just publicly squirted yourself with cafeteria water."

"Maybe my school could've used one of those things," I said.

"Every high school could. And every law firm, hedge fund, and government office, while we're at it."

"You should start a business," I said. "Though it might be a hard sell. There can't be a huge market for faulty water fountains."

"I'm afraid not," Alexandra said. "Tell me about the hierarchy at your school."

"Oh, it's exactly like medieval Europe. Except worse. Back then, at least, the serfs were protected by their overlords."

"Are you a serf?" Alexandra asked.

"Metaphorically, yes," I said.

"What about Elise?"

"Yeah. Same as me."

I needed to change the subject. Quick. Scanning the room, I pounced on the first thing I saw.

"Your shoes," I said, "are the exact color of a Splenda packet. I just noticed."

Alexandra thoughtfully revolved an ankle. "I'm not sure how I feel about them. It was a risky purchase. Yellow, you know. Hard color to wear."

"Everything is yellow here," I observed. "The paint. The bedding."

"Always has been," Alexandra said. "Always yellow."

"I wonder if my Splenda tolerance has dropped," I wondered. "Since I haven't had it in two weeks. You build up a tolerance, you know. We were talking about it the other day at breakfast, me and Victoria and Haley. We went around the table admitting how many Splenda packets we put in our coffee and tea. You wouldn't believe how much Haley uses."

"That's interesting that you all use the same sweetener."

"Well, everyone uses Splenda. Haley uses eight packets. That seems a little extreme, even to me."

"Do you like the taste of it? I find those sweeteners to have a bitter aftertaste."

"Splenda doesn't have an aftertaste," I said. "Actually, it doesn't have a taste, period. It's just sugar without the flavor of sugar. Pure sweetness. I use three packets for an iced tea, or more if the tea has a lot of lemon in it. I can't even taste it if I use only one. My mom always had a box lying around, though I never saw her use it. She doesn't have a sweet tooth."

I couldn't gauge whether Alexandra knew what I was doing. What subject I was avoiding.

"After I finished my mom's box, I started buying it on my own," I rambled on. "Then she realized what was going on, and suddenly I wasn't allowed to buy it anymore. It was like finding cigarettes in my jacket pocket or something—she'd just throw it out—so I took packets from Starbucks whenever I ordered coffee. Handfuls of them. I kept them in a little silk Chinese pouch, and if I forgot to bring the pouch to school with me, I couldn't eat lunch. It was a big deal, that pouch."

"Why couldn't you eat lunch?"

"Because it had to be consistent. We ate the same thing every day."

"You and—?"

"Elise," I said, with some irritation. "We ate a coffee yogurt with two Splendas stirred in and a green apple for lunch. If one of the items was missing, the whole routine would be thrown off. Like, if I just ate the yogurt without the apple, I'd end up feeling unsatisfied all afternoon and then I'd eat something bad to make up for it. I kept a supply of coffee yogurt and green apples in the fridge in case I forgot the pouch, so I could just come straight home after school and prepare the same thing I would have eaten earlier. It wasn't an ideal system, but at least it meant that I could stay on track."

"You must have gotten hungry when that happened."

I shrugged. "It didn't happen that often. Once a month, maybe. I'm not a forgetful person."

"What would happen if you were to eat something different for lunch?"

I considered this.

"This past February, one day I left my pouch at home. It was a horrible time of year. Valentine's Day right around the corner, the streets coated in dirty snow, everyone sick of bundling up in a smelly winter coat. I spent my whole morning thinking about lunch. Looking forward to it. Imagining myself sitting next to Elise with our identical meals, alternating tiny spoonfuls of yogurt with bites of tart, crunchy apple, and recapping our struggles and triumphs of the morning."

I could almost taste the food as I described it. Sweet and sour; crisp and creamy. The ideal contrast.

"Did you always eat with Elise?

"Always. Anyhow, on that day I realized I'd forgotten the pouch as soon as I got out of class before lunch period. It wasn't a big deal, though, because Elise always had extras on her. So I went to our lunch spot and waited for her."

"Where was your lunch spot? In the cafeteria?"

"What, in front of all those people? Our lunch spot was a little-used staircase covered in rough green carpeting where we could conduct our eating ritual in relative privacy. I waited and waited there, drumming my fingers against the tin lid of the yogurt container, wanting to peel it back. The halls were dry and overheated and stung my nostrils. I tried Elise on her cell phone, but nothing. She didn't pick up. I tried texting her, and when that didn't work, I just sat and typed random letters into my phone, desperate to look occupied as people walked past me in the hallway, glancing at my lunch and drawing the inevitable conclusion that I was a loser who had no one to eat with."

"That's a powerful feeling. To feel abandoned like that."

"Yeah. My appetite was gone, and I didn't have anywhere to go. Walking around by myself wasn't an option, since it would only mean that *more* people would see me alone. But I couldn't sit there much longer, and after a while I got up, threw out my yogurt, and went upstairs to the third-floor bathroom."

I hated thinking about this.

"The library is the only thing on the third floor, and no one ever uses that bathroom during lunch. It was my last-resort oasis. I went into the largest stall, closed the door, and sat with my apple, revolving it in my hands but not eating it. Eating it would have made noise, and if somebody came in to use the bathroom and heard me eating? Ugh, no."

Alexandra stayed statue-still as she listened to me.

"By seventh period I still had no idea where Elise was, and my stomach was grumbling loud enough in class to provoke stares from the people sitting next to me. To get through it, I chewed gum and concentrated with all of my might on the stockpile of coffee yogurts awaiting me at home. I pictured the smooth, plastic containers stacked in the fridge. I reviewed the nutrition stats in my head: 150 calories per yogurt, with 2.5 grams of fat, 7 grams of protein, 25 grams of carbs, and 25 grams of sugar. I imagined the resistance that my spoon would meet with when I dipped it into the thick, mocha-colored substance. I repeated it to myself like a mantra, *Don't worry, Zoe. You're going to get your lunch. Don't worry, Zoe, you're going to get your lunch. Don't worry. It's waiting for you, cold and perfect and sweet. As soon as school gets out, you'll get your lunch.*

"I was ecstatic when the bell finally rang. I practically sprinted home, skidding over ice-caked pavements and not caring what people thought of me. I ran up the stairs to my apartment building, unlocked the door, beelined for the kitchen and stopped."

I hated remembering this part.

"My mom was sitting on the kitchen table," I said. "Waiting for me."

I closed my eyes. All feelings faded in memory except for embarrassment. Alexandra waited for me to continue the story.

"My silk pouch was in front of her, empty. Each packet of

Splenda, fourteen, twenty, I don't know, was lined up on the kitchen table, like forensic evidence. Like contraband. And she just started saying the same thing over and over again. She said, 'I'm very angry, Zoe. You lied to me again, and I'm very, very angry with you.' "

It was hard to breathe. Air seemed to be entering my body from a narrow tube.

"She made me pour each packet down the garbage disposal in front of her," I said. "Individually."

I shut my eyes and watched thin streams of white powder drift into the black rubber hole at the center of the sink. My fingers had grown sticky with fake-sugar; I shook with rage and humiliation as I emptied the packets. My mother stood with her hands clenched, livid at me for lying and disobeying her. My stomach lurched with hunger pains.

"I don't think I've ever wanted anything more than I wanted that meal," I said, opening my eyes again. The room seemed whiter than usual, and I had to steady myself by putting both palms facedown on the sofa. "Not any food, but that exact food. Every cell in my body anticipated that specific meal. The yogurt. The apple. I did not want anything else. I did not want to break my routine. I would rather have not eaten at all."

"Why?" Alexandra asked.

"Because. It was a certainty, and I liked it that way. I liked my apple and my yogurt at lunch. I liked rewarding myself with low-fat ice cream. I liked knowing that I didn't have to think about food or wonder what to eat or how much. It was like wearing a uniform to school, something I always secretly wished for. I didn't have to devote a single thought to it. There were no questions. Ever."

None.

"Nothing else in my life," I went on, "was like that. I woke up and got out of bed every morning with no idea of what the day would bring. As soon as I got to the bathroom to brush my teeth, it started: Was my skin going to be good today, or would it break out? Would I have to spend the whole day angling my face away from people so they wouldn't have to stare at a boiling patch of acne? Did my breath smell? Would I have to play basketball in PhysEd? Would my deodorant work? Would I get sweat patches in my underarms before lunch? What if I accidentally scratched a zit during Spanish class and it started bleeding, and the boy next to me points to my forehead and hands me a Kleenex? What if Elise was sick again and didn't come to school? What if I got my period and bled through my pants? What if I have razor burn on my legs?"

I was speaking from experience, not hypothetically.

"These questions," I told Alexandra, "are shooting through my head every day before I even spit out the toothpaste in my mouth. Do you understand?

She nodded. I was gripping the sofa too tightly.

"It. Does. Not. Stop."

Removing my hands from the leather upholstery, I transferred them to my thighs, which I proceeded to squeeze as tightly as a stress ball.

"But that's not all," I went on. "There's also the fact that my best friend is perfect. Literally perfect. My best friend is a tall, lanky, beautiful girl that everyone falls in love with on first sight."

I felt a sharp pain. My nails were carving half-moons into my thighs. I'd been clutching my legs so tightly that my fingernails had broken through the fabric of the leggings and were pushing against my skin. Almost as soon as I registered the pain in my legs, it disappeared.

"When I finally figured out that there was something within my ability to control, I controlled it."

I collapsed back into the sofa, winded. The light in the room seemed to be growing brighter and brighter. What time was it?

"I see," Alexandra said.

There were tears in my eyes, but they did not feel like tears. They felt like hot water or Tabasco sauce. They scorched my skin and dribbled onto my leggings. Hot and sour tears. I trained my eyes on Alexandra's shoes in order to avoid making eye contact, but the sight of the bright yellow material was beginning to make me feel off-kilter in a different way. I put my head in my hands and squeezed my eyes shut. Velvet blackness swept around me like a curtain, but Alexandra's yellow Mary Janes were imprinted in my mind. I could feel the sticky paste of damp Splenda on my fingers and hear the sound of the garbage disposal churning. It was a terrifying sound. Back in the kitchen at home, doubled over with panic and stomach cramps, I saw my mother's face, taut with anger, as she plucked the kitchen scissors from the butcher block and snipped my silk pouch in half, then into quarters. A cloud of white powder floated to the counter as the last bits of Splenda evaporated into thin air.

"No more of this, Zoe," my mom said.

*Of what?* I wanted to scream. My mother had never understood what I was doing, or why I was doing it. She had never asked. She had never known.

"Do you hear what I am saying to you?" she whispered, her voice thick with fury. But I couldn't speak. She grabbed my wrists and pinned them, forcing me to look into her eyes.

"You will not," she said, and then dropped my hands, trembling. "You will not lie to me again, Zoe."

The scene spun out like a broken reel, and midnight poured itself around me. Blackness again. A high buzzing sound filled my head, and I was aware of a cold, twinkly feeling radiating from the place right behind my ears. Like a TV set unplugged from the wall, everything went quiet.

I wasn't sure what was happening, so I lay still, breathing fast but no longer crying. Something soft and warm covered my body. My feet felt different; wiggling my toes, I realized that I was not wearing shoes. When had that happened? The darkness around me looked different, not too black anymore but more like the color of a storm cloud. Was it safe to open my eyes? I tried, with great caution, to do so, but nothing happened. I tried again and couldn't do it.

My eyes were already open. A shape materialized above me. A voice was connected with the shape. But the sensations didn't fully overlap, and I couldn't tell whether it was Angela or Alexandra who hovered nearby. The voice sounded like Angela, but the face looked like Alexandra. Black hair. Skinny limbs. Someone brought another blanket and gently unfolded it on my body. But it wasn't the white afghan I was holding before, and I couldn't *feel* the blanket even though I could *see* that it was on top of me. I heard people talking. Not sentences, just words.

*Under observation . . .*
*Triggered by . . .*
*Be fine, though we ought to . . .*
*A memory . . .*

Then the words disintegrated into sounds, and the effort of decoding became too great. Either Angela or Alexandra put a hand on my forehead. I closed my eyes again and surrendered to viscous sleep.

# [DAY NINETEEN]

**Breakfast**
Chicken broth (2 cups)
White toast with butter (2 pieces)
Orange juice (8 oz.)

**Lunch**
Chicken broth (2 cups)
White toast with butter (2 pieces)
Hot lemon water (8 oz.)

**Dinner**
Chicken broth (2 cups)
White toast with butter (3 pieces)
Hot lemon water (8 oz.)

# [day twenty]

*Ever wondered what* it feels like to fall into a volcano? If so, allow me to recommend a panic attack. A panic attack is what happened to me yesterday afternoon in the middle of therapy. I was telling Alexandra about a fight I'd had with Mom when I began, quite suddenly, to feel dizzy and hot, as though I'd plummeted through the office floor into a pit of lava. I seemed to be falling for a long time, and just as I approached the molten flames at the bottom of the pit, everything went dark.

How's that for a waking nightmare?

I woke up several hours later in a lamp-lit room, covered in blankets, with a nurse helicoptering over me. Alexandra was there, too — or it might have been Angela. In that state, I couldn't have distinguished a pineapple from a kiwi.

A few hours later I was allowed to go back to my room and rest. With Caroline otherwise occupied, I had almost a full day of privacy. In theory. I say "in theory" because I have not, in truth, had a *second* of privacy in my bedroom. At all times there are ten faces staring at me from atop Caroline's dresser. Ten faces gazing upon every banal activity I embark upon. When I put on my striped socks, I feel their eyes. When I untangle a knot in my hair, I feel them, too. When I undress for a shower—you get the idea. It sounds funny, but a photograph has a distinct presence, and ten photographs are almost unbearably intrusive. Even if the photographs are of a child.

Still, I would never ask her to remove the pictures. I would never be that brave. Shuddering under their surveillance, I felt the limits of my existence vividly, almost physically, as though I were handcuffed.

At dinner time, Angela brought me a tray loaded with plain white toast, soup, and hot water, which I picked at in bed, like an invalid. I hadn't eaten white toast in years, and I was surprised at how sweet it tasted; almost like angel-food cake. The other girls were at dinner, and my room was silent as a crypt except for the crunch and slurp of my eating.

Toast reminds me of midnight snacks and hotel breakfasts. Many years ago, I sat in the kitchen of our house watching my older brother make toast in the broiler. The square footage of our kitchen was so dinky that my mother refused to buy an actual toaster. ("Not enough counter space," she said, confirming my theory that *all* moms *everywhere* are obsessed with counter space.) I developed a scientific interest, that morning, in observing Harry prepare his toast. I must have been eight years old. He was crouched by the stove, bouncing on his heels and waiting for the bread to hit that perfect shade of golden-brown doneness. "Remember to flip it," I told him. People always forget that a toaster does all the work, but a broiler only does half of it.

"That's what I hate about toasting in a broiler," he said, tapping the oven glass. "Touching the soft side of the bread that doesn't face the flames. It feels creepy."

When the smell of toast was in the air, Harry yanked the broiler door open and pulled out the tray. One side of the toast was done. As he reached for the bread and flipped it over, a look of disgust crossed his face. It only lasted a second, but I remember being pleased, because it meant that he had been telling the truth about his aversion.

"Yech, it's like touching mold," he said.

I miss Harry, too.

Angela asked, this morning, if I would like to talk with my mother on the phone after the panic attack. A special exception to the rule, she said. I declined—not to be vengeful, but because I have nothing to say. It happened and it's over. Done. Finished. I'd like to forget about it—to smooth it over like a cowlick. I don't want to talk about the memory that triggered it, and the rest of the time I was unconscious. So there you have it.

# [day twenty-one]

*I was late to breakfast.* When I arrived, Devon had taken the vacant seat at Victoria and Haley's table. The only chair left stood between Jane and Caroline, and directly across from Brooke.

Splendid.

Victoria gave me a helpless glance as I entered and sat down. *Are you okay?* she mouthed. I nodded. Caroline stood to pour ice water for Brooke, Jane, and herself, conspicuously skipping my glass. I poured my own ice water and waited quietly for Devon to call us up for food as they talked amongst themselves. When it was our table's turn, I trudged over to the sideboard, steeling myself for what awaited. Devon, with an apron tied around her waist, happily accepted my plate and dug a spoon into the serving tray. Although we are still allowed to serve ourselves, nobody does so anymore because no matter what size portion you take, Devon always adds more. If I take one slice of toast, she ups the ante with another slice. If I serve myself a dollop of almond butter, she triples the dollop. Now I just hand over my plate and let her do it. It's easier that way.

"Southwestern omelet," Devon announced, depositing a floppy oval of egg onto my plate. I detected red peppers, onions, chives, and cheddar cheese from the steaming, pillow-shaped object. A cube of cornbread was added to the plate, and immediately commenced soaking up excess egg juice like a sponge. I prodded the bread away from the omelet with my finger.

"How're you feeling, Zoe?" Devon asked.

"Fine."

Did they tell Devon about my panic attack? I hate the idea. The last thing I need is extra attentiveness from her.

I returned to my solitary perch at the table and focused on the wet raft of cornbread, alternately preparing for and avoiding the task ahead of me. After nearly three weeks, I still can't adjust to the sensation of packing such large amounts of food down my throat. It has indelicate effects on my digestion. Worst of all, what if I get used to it? It is inconceivable that I will eat a tenth as much as I'm eating here once I return to normal life. I watched the food on my plate carefully, as though it might—if given the proper encouragement—evaporate all on its own.

Spoiler alert: It didn't.

Out of habit and politeness, I waited for everyone to return to her seat before I began eating. Not that it mattered here. (I also cover my mouth when I yawn or sneeze, hold the door for others, put my napkin in my lap, and leave the bathroom in spotless condition. Again, not that it matters here.)

Caroline sat down next to me, followed by Jane. The smell of eggs was overpowering. For some people, food is a comforting thing—a way to soothe bad moods and feel better instantly, if temporarily. But for me, it doesn't work this way. For me, a bite of ice cream is not just a bite of ice cream, but also a threat: the threat that I'll want more ice cream than just that one bite, and the threat that I'll keep wanting it and wanting it until I can think of nothing except ice cream, and about what would happen if I ate the ice cream, and about how disappointed I'd be with myself afterward.

Some people find it impossible to be unhappy while eating. I suppose I am the exact opposite.

Waiting for the others to return proved a mistake. As soon as Brooke returned to the table, a horrifying charade of consumption played itself out before me: She bent down and crammed food into her mouth, throwing back gulps of water to push it down her throat. Jane and Caroline seemed thoroughly accustomed to the performance, and they embarked upon their own strange eating rituals without a second glance at their tablemate.

I shrunk into my velvet seat, smushing my cornbread into the shape of a pancake with a spoon. I cut the pancake into eighths, then lifted a slice to eat. The voyage from my plate to my mouth seemed to take years. Between Brooke and the cornbread, there was nothing in my field of vision that didn't act as a potential enemy.

When it arrived, the cornbread tasted like wet paper towels and undercooked eggs. I swallowed and put my fork down.

Except for Brooke, the other girls seemed to have similar opinions.

"At least the portions are getting smaller," Jane was telling Caroline. "They've been getting progressively smaller every day. Have you noticed?

I looked down at the football-sized omelet. Was it smaller? It didn't look smaller. It looked mammoth.

But Caroline concurred. "It's hard to detect because the change is so gradual," she said sagely.

This didn't make sense to me. The more we ate, the more food our stomachs could handle. Why would the portions be getting smaller? I gazed longingly at the other table, where Victoria was whipping Haley's hand with a stringy piece of caramelized onion. *Never again,* I told myself, cursing my seat. I am *never* going to be late again. Brooke furiously speared her last chunk of omelet and chewed at least thirty times. When finished, she wiped her mouth and stared straight at me through smudged glasses.

"Stop staring," she said.

"What?"

"Stop staring at me."

"I wasn't—"

"You were. You're *always* looking at me."

"I—"

"You look at me as though *I'm* the one who's a freak," she went on. "You, of all people! Given *your* history, I can't bel—"

Brooke stopped on a dime and shut her mouth tight.

"*My* history?"

"Never mind."

"No, tell me just what you mean by *my* history!"

"You know exactly what I'm talking about."

I couldn't believe what I was hearing. Brooke was the weirdo, not me.

Caroline and Jane stared at me with undisguised contempt. *They planned this*, I thought. They saved the seat specifically to torture me.

Was I imagining it?

Ignoring Brooke's speech, I bent to face my waterlogged cornbread and gelatinous eggs, wishing I could hide beneath the table like a five-year-old at Thanksgiving. Even my coffee was cold. Somehow I'd have to coax myself into swallowing the entire heap with the eyes of my tablemates trained curiously on me.

A white envelope was visible through the slot. I squinted harder. Was it an envelope I'd seen before? Impossible to say. Viewed through a quarter-inch opening in a small box, all standard white envelopes look the same. I straightened up and flicked a piece of lint off the top of the red box as I waited outside for my session to begin. By now I'd learned a few things about the red box:

One, that it was easier to discern the contents if I kept one eye closed while I peeked inside.

Two, the box never contained more than one envelope at a time.

Three, the envelope was always positioned facedown, with the address hidden from sight. These facts, so far, had not been disproven.

The door swung open. I nodded to Alexandra, whose appearance every day was another invitation to play the color game. Today the game was hard, because she wore no belt, no jewelry, no hat, and no scarf. For shoes, she'd selected simple white leather sandals. As we took our respective seats in the bleach-white room, I wondered if Alexandra had—was it possible?—forgotten to add any color at all to her getup. I hoped not. If so, I'd have to revise the rules of the game. And I really hate changing the rules of a game.

"Tea? Water?" she offered.

"No, thanks," I said. We assumed our positions on the chair and couch.

Alexandra smiled and folded her hands across one knee. The gesture revealed what I'd been searching for: Ten nails were painted electric tangerine. The color of deer-hunting caps.

We faced off in silence for a moment while I squirmed for a way to broach the subject.

"Have you ever seen a nature documentary about Africa?" I asked, still distracted by her nails.

"More than one," she said. "Probably a hundred. I have two boys, so . . ."

"So you know the territory. Nature movies were the only common ground I had with my brother, as far as TV-watching went. So we watched a lot of them together. I can still tell you everything you need to know about bush elephants and cheetahs and African hunting dogs. And hyenas, too. Did you know they eat dry bones? Hyenas?"

Alexandra shook her head.

"Anyway you've seen those movies, so you know what happens to zebras."

"Remind me," Alexandra said.

"Okay. Every nature documentary about Africa has a zebra scene in it," I said. "Or a variation of a zebra scene. It's the one where you see a pack of nice, gentle zebras going down to the river for a drink of water. Usually they get a wide shot of the zebras so you can see how many there are."

"I seem to remember scenes involving zebras and rivers," Alexandra said.

"And alligators," I said. "Don't forget the alligators. Everything starts out fine until one poor zebra chooses the wrong spot along the riverbank for his afternoon drink. For this part, the camera zooms in close. Too close. We watch the zebra bend his long neck down to the water's surface, thirsty after a stressful day on the open plains. His nostrils flare in the heat. Suddenly, without warning—BAM—an alligator leaps up from beneath the water and clenches its jaws around the zebra's neck."

I shivered.

"Predator meets prey," Alexandra said.

"And then the alligator is literally eating the zebra in midair. Can you imagine? Being eaten in midair?"

Alexandra paused, squinted, and then shook her head. "Nope," she said. "I just tried. I can't imagine it."

"Well, I can. Easily."

"Do you identify with the zebra or the alligator?"

"The zebra," I said. "Jesus. What do you think I am, a psycho? Who identifies with the alligator?"

She ignored my question. "So you feel like a prey animal," she said. "Vulnerable. Tell me why."

*Why* was an easy question to answer. I explained to her about the breakfast incident. About the strange things Brooke had said to me. As I did this, a flicker of unease crossed Alexandra's face, and her jaw grew taut.

"Would you mind telling me again what Brooke said?" Alexandra asked, flipping to a fresh sheet on her legal pad. "Her exact words, if you can? Verbatim."

Her tone was different. Like a cross-examining attorney.

"It's hard to remember the exact words," I said. "I wasn't taking notes or anything. The whole thing took me by surprise. But she said, I think, that how dare I look at her as though she were crazy, given my history."

"'Given your history'?" Alexandra repeated.

I nodded.

Looking even more perturbed, she scribbled something down on her notepad, then emphatically crossed it out and scribbled something else. Ten neon orange nails flew above the page. She paused, pen hovering, and looked up at me.

"This isn't the first time that you've had a hostile interaction with one of the girls," she said. "The first was when Caroline asked you to justify your presence at Twin Birch. The second time was when Brooke accused you of stealing her dress. The third was when she accused you of staring at her in a way that made her uncomfortable."

"*Hostile interaction* makes it sound mutual," I said. "It wasn't mutual. *They* were the aggressors."

"Do you see a pattern?"

"Between what?"

"Between these interactions. A commonality."

I did not see a commonality.

"Each time you've had a conflict with Brooke or Caroline," Alexandra said, "it's because one of them appears to feel bothered by your presence, or is suspicious of you. And each time, from your perspective, the conflict seems completely unmotivated and random."

"Are you saying that I've been threatening them?"

"No, no. I'm saying that, for whatever reason, you strike them as a threatening presence."

"I don't see how this is my fault," I said. "They're both hypersensitive."

"Be that as it may," Alexandra said, "can you think of any reason why Brooke or Caroline would see you as a threat?"

A fiery pit was developing in my stomach. A distress signal.

"No."

"Let's go at this from a different angle. Let's revisit that first conflict, when Caroline asked you why you were at Twin Birch. Do you think she was genuinely curious about the reasons why you might be here?"

"I don't know. I guess so."

"And are you?"

"Am I what?" I said.

"Curious," Alexandra replied. "Have you asked yourself why you're at Twin Birch?"

*All the goddamn time, you moron*, I wanted to scream. I controlled myself.

"It wasn't my decision to come here," I said quietly.

"That might be another reason to think about the question. A very good reason, maybe."

Her tone had the air of conveying a lot of information in a coded manner. Too much information for me to absorb. Information that I was not equipped to understand.

Alexandra continued, "This might be harder for you than you think, but I think it's also going to be easier. For example, your letters to Elise—"

"What does Elise have to do with Brooke?" I interrupted.

"Quite a lot."

"No," I said. "There is no connection between those two things."

"You seem upset that I've suggested a link," Alexandra said.

She leaned forward, hands clasped in the prayer position. "Zoe," she said, her voice alarmingly gentle. "You're here at Twin Birch for a reason."

*Nothingness.*

"Have you talked to my mother?" I asked.

"Many times."

"And she said—"

"You're here for a reason, Zoe. I need you to try and understand that."

Her lipstick was freshly applied. In the white office, it looked like a spot of blood on snow. Alexandra got up and fetched a blanket from the cabinet—I guess I was shivering. I hate her ability to notice every little thing. I hate being watched like a lab rat. She put the blanket next to me on the sofa. I did not touch it.

"This is something we can work on together," she went on. "Understanding why you are here."

*There's nothing the matter with me. Why can't anyone see that?*

A knock at the door alerted us to the arrival of another patient.

"That's Jane, and she's early," Alexandra said. "Please, Zoe, sit down. We have a few more minutes."

"No," I said, already throwing my full weight against the door. "We don't."

# [DAY TWENTY-TWO]

*I opened my eyes* to a sky the color of concrete. A dismal day for a dismal girl.

My legs have changed shape. A few weeks ago, I could stand upright, feet together, and feel a gap between my thighs as broad as a cell phone. Now, I'd be lucky to fit a quarter into the same area. My stomach has acquired a soft bulge which makes me look as though I'm three months pregnant. That's not a figure of speech. When you gain weight quickly, it all goes straight to your stomach and redistributes over time. I've stopped looking in the mirror when I brush my teeth or wash my face at night. What's the point? I know what I look like. There is physical matter where there used to be air.

I see it in other girls, too. Caroline's elbows are no longer sharp enough to cut butter. The brittleness has vanished from Haley's face.

Other changes have occurred. There are fewer chattering teeth. When did it peter out? I don't know; my own teeth never chattered. I was never thin enough for that. But the rest of the patients were, and it occurred to me as we warmed up this morning that the sound had diminished to barely anything. Instead of crustaceans scrabbling across a rocky beach, there was quiet. Not even the sound of a lost hermit crab or two.

I've developed a writing callus on my right middle finger. Composing long letters to Elise has created a bump big enough to alter the silhouette of my hand. I'm expanding in every physical dimension. Inch by inch, day by day.

Still, the tippy-toe end of my third week at Twin Birch seems an occasion worthy of celebration. If I had a calendar to tack to my bedroom wall here, I'd cross off each day one by one in thick black Magic Marker X's. I'd host a celebration as soon as half the days were marked off. The drive home from a destination always seems shorter than the drive there, and I'm hoping that a similar logic will apply to this situation.

Dear Elise,

"Have you lost a lot of weight recently?"

Those were her exact words. The date is lost to me, but I remember that the outside stairs of our school building were still crusted over in layers of ice, so it must have been this past winter. January or February. We were making our way carefully down the steps for a coffee run during one of those infernal twenty-minute breaks between classes, and I was aware, as I was always aware, that somebody was watching as we walked. At the foot of the steps stood Katie—yes, the same Katie who had scornfully informed you, the first week of freshman year, that Alex's note was a joke—with her hands stuffed into a North Face, smelling lightly and sophisticatedly of the cigarette that she'd just smoked around the corner. I had the distinct sense, as I stepped gingerly down the icy steps, that she wanted me to fall.

*Have you lost a lot of weight recently?* is usually a compliment. The way Katie said it, however, ruled out that interpretation. You reached the bottom of the stairs before I did, and you must have accidentally caught her eye. That was a mistake. Eye contact is an invitation to engage, and engagement with upperclassmen had never been a good thing in our experience. In a casually neutral tone that was loud enough to carry well beyond the immediate circle of bystanders, Katie openly appraised you:

"Have you lost a lot of weight recently?"

Caught by surprise, you stammered.

Katie grinned frostily in response and declined to repeat herself. Her silence spoke loud and clear: *You heard me*, it said. Her friends, meanwhile, looked at you with scientific objectivity, as though you were a lab sample. I did my best to glare at Katie from my precarious position on the stairs, but she didn't budge her line of sight from you.

"Oh, not really," you said, fiddling with the buttons on your navy pea coat. Before you could say another word, I looped my arm protectively through yours and pulled you away, muttering something urgent about coffee. We should have walked slowly—that was our second mistake—because it would have suggested, at least, that we weren't running away from Katie. But my flight instincts overruled any shred of dignity that I might have salvaged for us, and within seconds we'd reached the end of the block and turned a corner.

"What *was* that?" I said.

"What was what?" you asked, your face a mask of bewilderment.

"Katie. What was she doing? I hate when people ask dishonest questions. I mean, obviously you've lost weight. She *knew* that. She just wanted you to admit it in public, to embarrass you. Just like that time with the note."

"I guess it wasn't so nice of her."

"Not so nice?" I said, fuming. "God, I *hate* people sometimes."

We arrived at Starbucks, and you held the door open for me, welcoming a blast of warm, coffee-smelling air. The line was long, and to pass the time, you began removing strands of pale blond hair from your wool coat. "Ugh, winter static," you said, pulling away the stray hairs. There were more than usual this time.

I was still mad about Katie, and I didn't understand why you weren't.

"It's not the first time that's happened," you said simply when I brought it up.

"With Katie?"

"No, other people."

"Who?" I asked.

We ordered our coffees and went to the bar to doctor them with the appropriate amounts of soy milk.

"Don't people ask you about it?" you said, wrapping

your hands around the hot paper cup as we exited the store. "Don't people tell you that you're too thin? Or that you've lost too much weight?"

"No," I said. "No one except my mom and Harry. Do people say stuff to you?"

"All the time."

A spasm of jealousy rippled through me.

"It's annoying," you went on. "I mean, what am I supposed to say back? 'Yes, I have lost weight, as a matter of fact.' And then what? Am I supposed to sit down and toss back a cheeseburger because someone thinks I'm too thin?" You took a sip of coffee. "I mean, what does anyone hope to accomplish by saying that?"

My pace quickened. How come nobody had told *me* that I looked too thin? What did that mean? I summoned an image of our food schedule in my head and mentally scanned it for ways to eliminate fifty—no, a hundred—calories from my day. I had to catch up with you before you lost even more weight. *No low-fat ice cream*, I decided. I did not deserve any kind of treat at this rate of progress.

"Why are we walking so fast?" you said.

"Oh," I said, slowing down. "Sorry. I didn't realize."

"Zoe, you're not upset, are you?"

I shrugged. Your eyes widened in unease at the idea that we were on a different plane of existence, and you pulled to a halt, laying a gentle hand on my arm.

"Look, you know it's a matter of distribution, right?

I'm taller. My bones are bigger. They stick out more, so I look bonier. You're tiny, all the way around—"

You spun me around in a 360-degree turn to illustrate.

"Tiny," you concluded. "It's just the way we lose weight as individuals. I look skinnier, whereas you look teenier. Look at it another way. No matter how much weight you ever gain, you'll never look fat. It's physically impossible. You're petite, like a little French ballerina. Your limbs are small. Whereas me, if I let myself go, I'd look like a defensive back."

"I wish I had long, lanky arms," I said. "Sinewy. Like Gwyneth Paltrow's."

"Yeah, well, I wish I were itty-bitty like you. You know what I realized the other day? I'll never be able to sit in my boyfriend's lap. Not that I *have* a boyfriend, but if I did, I wouldn't be able to. Because I'm too tall. Isn't that horrible? He'll never be able to pick me up and twirl me around, or do anything cute with me. I'm too big."

"Well, I wish we could switch," I said. "I wish I could be you."

"Story of my life," you said. "I wish I could be you."

We linked arms and squeezed tight, relieved to see that Katie and her friends had dispersed from the front of our school. After making our usual plans for lunch and splitting off to go to class, I turned impulsively to watch you walk through the crowded hallway and performed a mental exercise that I sometimes do, which is to look at you the way an outsider would. I did this as students bobbed and pushed around me, noting your twig-like legs, ballet flats, and ponytail of blond hair. The ponytail, I discerned, was not as thick as it once was. In the time it took to get from Starbucks back to school, your coat had become covered, once again, with strands of blond hair. I wondered if anyone but me would notice.

I don't know why I keep sending you these letters.

Zoe

# [Day TWenty-Three]

*I woke up on* the right side of the bed. Against the odds — the odds being curried-tofu salad on brown bread and fried zucchini blossoms — it even lasted through lunch, possibly because Brooke was absent. Was I happy? No. But I felt optimistic. I told myself that the hard part was over. I even had an intuition that something good might happen. A treat of some kind, or a surprise — a letter from Elise, or the discovery that I'd stopped gaining weight.

I did indeed get a surprise. But not the kind I expected.

The morning's cheery omens carried over into cooking class, where we made Carrot Crack Fries. Along with the kale chips, these are my favorite things I've learned how to make. They're basically french fries made out of carrots, but healthy. And addictive — hence the name. Aside from the sugar-melting smell of baking carrots, the atmosphere was duly improved by Brooke's disappearance. Missing Intake, warm-up, and Activity was highly unusual, though, and as the morning wore on, the mood darkened as we all began to wonder where she'd gone. Something was up, and it wasn't until lunch that we found out what it was.

Angela made the announcement. She entered the room and waited while we transferred the heavy fry-laden serving dishes to the side tables, then supplanted Devon's place at the front of the room.

"Good afternoon, ladies," she began. "I'm here to make a brief announcement."

Five pairs of ears perked up.

"Brooke," Angela said, "is no longer with us. Due to patient confidentiality, we won't be able to discuss the reasons for her departure. However, you're encouraged to share your thoughts with Alexandra during your regular scheduled sessions or during open office hours. She'll be here until dinner tonight. Thank you, and bon appétit."

She nodded to Devon and left the room.

Five pairs of eyes grew wide with bewilderment.

An inner *Hallelujah!* erupted inside of me, though I was careful not to demonstrate my joy. Without adding any comments of her own, Devon herded us into the dining room for lunch, leaving us to speculate about Brooke amongst ourselves. Nobody, it seemed, had a clue what had happened to her.

**Carrot Crack Fries to Commemorate Sudden Disappearances**

3 large carrots

2 tbsp. oil (use safflower, peanut, or coconut oil)

Sea salt

1 tbsp. maple syrup

Preheat oven to 450 degrees. Cut carrots into french-fry shapes (use a sharp knife), then toss in oil, salt, and maple syrup. Spread out on a cookie sheet and cook for 35–45 minutes, until slightly browned.

Eat by the handful to celebrate the retreat of an enemy.

"It's not working," I informed Alexandra after lunch. "As of today I've spent 18.75 hours in therapy, and I do not feel 18.75 percent better about anything in my life."

"That makes you a very tough critic," she said. "Do you expect therapy to make you feel better?"

"Yes. Of course I do. What else is it good for?"

"Well," she said. "It can help you learn things about yourself."

"And what if those things make a person less happy?" I asked. "Is that progress?"

Alexandra crossed her legs, adjusted her watch strap (cobalt-blue), and redirected the conversation.

"How are you doing for supplies?"

"Fine," I said slowly. My mind returned back to my room, to the half-depleted white box beneath my bed. I mentally scanned its contents. "I have plenty of envelopes and enough note cards to last. Victoria keeps stealing pens to draw temporary tattoos on Haley and forgetting to return them, but I only need one pen, so."

"Let me know if you need more."

"I like having only one pen," I said. "It's the same principle with hair bands. If I only have one around my wrist, I never lose sight of it. But give me twelve hair bands and I'll lose them all in ten seconds."

I was biding my time before addressing the Brooke question. I didn't want to seem overeager.

"Scarcity increases value," Alexandra agreed. "Have you ever tried buying asparagus out of season?"

"Yeah, it costs like three thousand dollars per pound."

"Exactly. It's the same reason we value beauty so highly, as humans."

"Because it's scarce?" I asked.

"Because it's scarce. You're still writing letters to Elise, I see."

My foot twitched of its own accord.

"You seem a little impatient today," Alexandra observed neutrally. "Is everything okay?"

"I think you can probably guess why I'm impatient," I said.

Once again, I can't *stand* when adults feign ignorance. They're always lecturing teenagers about not playing dumb—about breaking the habit of inserting "like" between every other word—and yet here was Alexandra, pretending to be dumber than a bundle of socks.

"Do I have to ask?" I said.

Silence.

"Okay. Why did Brooke get sent home today?"

Alexandra's hand smoothed the already-smooth linen of her pants, and I wondered, for the first time, whether she might not be quite as cucumber-cool about the morning's events as she had seemed. It had all happened so rapidly. First Brooke was there, and then she wasn't.

"Was it drugs?" I speculated. "Did she have coke or Adderall or something?"

"As Angela mentioned this morning," Alexandra said, "Brooke acted in a way that endangered the welfare of the other girls here. That's all I can really say, Zoe, without infringing upon patient confidentiality."

"But I thought we were allowed to talk about anything in here," I protested. A new idea occurred to me: "Does it have to do with the stolen clothes?" I asked.

"Zoe."

"No," I persisted. "Something doesn't feel right about this. Has it happened before at Twin Birch? That a girl gets sent home?"

"Only once."

"What happened that time?" I asked, then reconsidered. "Never mind. I know you won't answer that."

"Perhaps we could talk about how Brooke's leaving makes you feel," Alexandra prompted. There are no dead ends with Alexandra. As soon as you hit a wall in conversation, she opens up a side door.

"It feels great," I said curtly. "She hated me, in case you hadn't noticed."

"I don't know that she *did* hate you, Zoe."

"It hardly matters now."

"It does," Alexandra said, "because Brooke is still making you unhappy despite the fact that she's gone."

Now I looked for my own side door. "Your watch is the color of an IHOP," I said, pointing to her wrist. It was true. Her watch was the lurid blue color of an IHOP roof.

Alexandra glanced at her wrist.

"Is IHOP really international?" I went on, overenthusiastic in my rerouting of the discussion. "I've never heard of an IHOP in Rome. Or Barcelona. Maybe it should be called NHOP. National House of Pancakes."

"Let's stay on track, Zoe."

"I used to order cinnamon-apple pancakes with whipped cream on top," I went on dreamily, remembering trips with Harry and Mom. I could feel the lightweight cutlery in my palm, and the heavy laminated menu with its endless combinations. The smell of fake syrup in the air. It was warm inside the restaurant. Our table was splashed with sunlight. . . .

"Are you happy?" Alexandra interrupted.

I drifted back into the present.

"No," I said. "I'm not happy at all."

She waited for more.

"I can barely stay focused," I said. "Every molecule in my body wants to be someplace else." I sniffed the air, hoping obscurely for a trace of the syrup smell. There was none. "If you want to know," I added, "I find it very upsetting that someone can just disappear into thin air, even if that person is psychotic."

"Brooke," Alexandra said. "What upsets you about her leaving?"

"She's gone, and we were given no warning. None. I'm not sure whether she left this morning or last night—or *Jesus*, in the middle of the night. And to drive it all home, you won't even tell us what she *did*."

"Is it important for you to know?"

"*Yes*, it's important," I said, writhing with exasperation. "It's important that I know because otherwise the *exact same thing could happen to me.*"

There it was. That was the truth.

Alexandra wrote it—or something—down on her notepad. A woozy feeling rushed into my stomach, mingling with the huge tofu sandwich I'd eaten for lunch.

"Can I lie down?" I asked abruptly, hoisting myself onto the couch without waiting for an answer. In my peripheral vision I saw Alexandra sit up in her chair, rigid with concern. "I'm not having another panic attack," I said. "I just feel sick."

I closed my eyes. Alexandra instructed me through a series of breathing exercises, which I attempted half-heartedly. Breathing exercises never made any sense to me, as a calming mechanism. There's a reason why breathing is automatic: It's so boring that everyone would forget to do it otherwise. Still, I obediently manipulated my lungs in the prescribed manner. The sickness didn't make sense. Shouldn't I feel fine now that Brooke is gone? There was nothing for me to worry about anymore—no mean comments, no accusations, no moon-faced girls skulking about and throwing looks in my direction.

Best of all, there were less than two weeks left before I could go home. And yet—*something* was the matter. I opened my eyes to the pale white ceiling. "It's upsetting," I finally said, "when someone just disappears."

# [day twenty-six]

*Getting bad news* when you least expect it is like drinking a beer on an empty stomach. Or at least, the one time I've made that mistake.

I've gotten bad news before, but this time was different. My head was elsewhere. My body was exhausted. Sleep has been impossible over the past few days, and even when I can snatch a few hours, my dreams are exhausting and unstoppable. I wake up feeling groggier than if I hadn't slept at all.

There are five girls left at Twin Birch. The table scraps of information that Alexandra offered about Brooke during our session added up to nothing, but I promised myself that I would find out what happened. The issue has been at the center of my thoughts, causing disruptions in every activity I attempt to complete. The hours tumble forth in a blur of errors and fumbles. I'm sure it's the reason I can't sleep. I was late to breakfast today and took a long time to choke down my oatmeal, which tasted of sawdust. Even Victoria became impatient with me, but I couldn't help it: My throat had closed up, and every swallow brought me close to wretching. In cooking class, we measured out ingredients for lavender shortbread cookies. The recipe was simple; there were only six ingredients to mix together. Nonetheless, I forgot to add flour to my batch, which resulted in a tray of cookies that were flatter than communion wafers and smelled like dish soap. I scraped them into the trash and asked permission to go upstairs to my room for a nap. Devon denied the request, and I plodded to lunch in a fog.

After therapy I finally had some free time, and I went upstairs to my room for forty-five minutes of sleep. Another doomed plan, it turned out: Caroline had the same idea, and when I got to the room she was already there, asleep, curled on her side and sucking her thumb. I almost screamed at the sight of her—I'd wanted so badly to be *alone*. To Caroline's credit, the thumb-sucking had diminished slightly since the beginning of the summer, no doubt thanks to Alexandra's work, but I still woke up on odd nights to the faint, telltale sound of skin meeting saliva. In most moods it didn't distract me from the more substantial challenge of sleep. Today, however, I almost imploded. Slipping under the covers, I put a pillow over my head like a surly teenager in a sitcom. Then I tried to fall asleep.

No sooner had I shut my eyes than I felt a pressure on my shoulder. *No*, I thought desperately, mentally willing the intruder to *go away*. The pressure returned—two fingers digging into soft flesh above my collar bone. I continued to feign sleep. Then the pillow shielding my head began to move—someone was *physically* pulling it away—and I found myself staring into the eyes of Jane, who levitated above me, holding a finger to her lips.

"Caroline's asleep," she whispered.

"So was I," I whispered back, making no effort to conceal my irritation. "You're breaking the rules. I *didn't* say that you could come in here."

Jane's face was impenetrable. "I need to talk to you," she said. "About Brooke."

I sat up. "Why?"

Brooke and Jane had been roommates. Now that Brooke was gone, Jane slept alone in their bedroom. When I passed their partly open door, I saw that half the room had been wiped clean of any human trace.

Jane gestured toward Caroline and motioned impatiently for me to follow her out the door. Her steps were loud and careless, and I realized that she didn't care whether or not she woke Caroline up—only about whether Caroline heard what she said. I got out of bed and followed her into the hallway.

"I wasn't sure whether I wanted to tell you," Jane began, tucking a lank strand of hair behind one ear.

"Tell me what?" I said.

"I'm getting there," she said. "I know why Brooke left."

"*How?*" I whispered.

"Does it matter?"

She held up her palm, signaling once more for me to shut up. *You're the one who lured me into the hallway*, I wanted to remind her.

But never mind. She was a spy bearing foreign intelligence, and it behooved me to listen.

"You're the reason she went home," Jane said.

I narrowed my eyes. "If this is a mind game you're playing—"

"It's not a mind game; I'm only telling you what I know. Brooke got into Alexandra's office and read your file. She might have read other files too; I'm not sure. She might have read mine for all I know, though there's nothing in there that she didn't already know."

The fear came from a point deep within my body—almost at the exact center of it.

"When did she—?" I asked.

"A week ago," Jane said. "Alexandra figured it out—I don't know how, but she did. She got Brooke to admit it during therapy a couple of days ago. And that was that. They didn't even wait for Brooke's parents to make the drive down from Maine—she was picked up by some relative who lives in Boston."

Caroline's fuzzy blond head poked out from the doorframe of our bedroom. "What're you guys doing?" she asked warily, her voice sandpapered with sleep.

"Nothing," Jane said. The intrusion of a third party signaled the end of the conversation to Jane, who looked me in the eye with an unspoken warning—*Don't tell anyone*—before she left.

Caroline's eyes darted back and forth between me and Jane's retreating form as I squeezed past my roommate into our bedroom. She wanted to talk, I could tell. But I had nothing whatsoever to tell her.

Dear Elise,

The way I see it, it's a chicken-and-egg matter: Did we start paying attention to food because we wanted to lose weight, or vice versa? At what point does interest morph into obsession? We started out life as kids, with normal kid-attitudes toward food. Meals were an annoying interruption of playtime, and they were to be dispatched as quickly as possible so we could go back outside. Eating was a tiresome necessity, like brushing our teeth or going to pee. I have zero memories of childhood meals. Food didn't interest me until my appetite became a problem.

Victoria says that an eating disorder is like a virus that won't leave your system, even when the symptoms subside. "I'll never eat a bite of food without regretting it," she said this morning, running her finger over the waxy rind of a tangerine.

"Isn't that the point of recovery?" Haley said. "I can't bear the thought that I'll be this way forever. That every calorie I ingest will signify a failure."

"You've bitten the poison apple," I said. "Or the poison tangerine."

"I can't even look at an apple without thinking, *ninety calories*," Victoria said.

"I think the point of recovery isn't to erase these thoughts," Haley said slowly, "but to be able to recognize them as false. Or harmful."

"Maybe," Victoria said. "But you'll always have the debate with yourself. You have to resign yourself to the fact that your brain will always judge you for what you put into your mouth." She started to peel her tangerine. "Take it from someone who's been dealing with this a long, long time."

I listened silently to these discussions, wondering where I fit into the whole picture.

"I think Devon puts sugar in our orange juice for extra calories," Haley said.

"You're a conspiracy theorist." I watched Victoria struggle with the tangerine for a minute before thumping it emphatically against the table. "Goddammit. I trimmed my nails too short, and now I can't peel this thing. My fingers are stubs. I'm like a bear pawing at a jar of honey."

"I'll do it," I said, taking the fruit from her. When I was finished peeling, I passed the little orb back to Victoria. "I don't want to gain any more weight," I said.

"Don't think of it that way."

"Yeah," Haley added. "Don't."

"You have to force yourself to be passive and follow every direction they give you; otherwise, you'll just have to do it again in a different, worse place. And then again after that."

This is Victoria's fifth time in treatment.

"It's sad," Haley said quietly, "that we can't eat and be happy at the same time."

"It's the saddest thing in the world."

*No*, I thought to myself. *Missing my best friend is the saddest thing in the world.*

I cried about it at breakfast and lunch, and I almost started crying all over again as we cleared our plates. Why now? I don't know. Your silence scares me to my core. What did I do? Are you mad at me?

If I don't scale back, I'm going to die of tear-induced dehydration.

Perhaps I should stop writing.

Sometimes I cry out of guilt. For the rest of these girls, guilt is a foreign feeling. I mean, what do sixteen-year-olds have to feel guilty about? Nothing. Usually. At Twin Birch, I can't escape the feeling that I'm a criminal. The idea creeps into my consciousness from a dozen angles, making it impossible to pinpoint the source.

The eyes in the photos on Caroline's dresser follow me accusingly. It may just be the fact of being here, at an institution, that does it. If I'm a prisoner, I must have committed a crime—right?

Day number twenty-nine. I feel like a pile of bricks. Heavy, unthinking, immobile.

I know that you won't write me back, but it doesn't mean I stop hoping to find a letter in the mailbox with your handwriting on the envelope.

Intimacy is a double-edged sword. You get close to someone, or closer—Victoria and Haley, for example— and your entire social landscape is suddenly rosier. You have an ally! A partner in crime! You share conspiratorial glances. The chorus from "All You Need Is Love" drifts through your mind. The "new friend" feeling is even more delightful than the "new crush" feeling—because, after all, a new friendship is reciprocal.

But there's another side of intimacy, and that's weakness. Vulnerability. The price you pay for being close to someone is that they can whip around, no warning, and knife you in the back. It happens to everyone.

Therapists offer a fake version of intimacy. Fake because it's one-sided. Have you ever asked therapists any personal questions? Don't even try it. They won't answer. The patient-therapist relationship is fake because one party is paying for it, and the intimacy that develops in therapy should never be mistaken for the genuine article.

You and I, by contrast, have the genuine article. No

amount of absence can take that away from us. Even if you never respond to a single letter I write, I trust in my gut that you read them. I do. I can see you holding these pages; I can picture you in your bedroom, the glasses you won't let anyone else see you wear slipping down your nose, unsealing the envelope with a red-painted fingernail and retrieving the folded pages from within. I hope my handwriting is legible.

When the sound of your voice grows dim in my head, I return to memories that I've stored up in my mind—some good, others not so good.

Today I am thinking about our cold-weather shower ritual. When was the last time we performed it? It must have been in late March this year because the night was not only icy but unseasonably so. The drugstores, I remember, were already stocking Easter candy, but there was still snow on the cars. Friday evening arrived, and our only plans were to watch TV and stir packets of sugar-free cocoa powder into china mugs. As a rule I preferred your rambling townhouse to my family's cramped apartment. But the antique radiators distributed sparsely among your rooms were no match for a Brooklyn winter, and we had to bury ourselves in down comforters just to keep from shivering. Your parents were out to dinner. When I skittered into the bathroom to take a pre-bedtime shower, the floor was a frozen pond beneath my feet.

When I finished, it was your turn. "Ready?" I called out from the shower. We had a choreography in place that was designed to minimize our exposure to the cold air. We'd perfected it at every sleepover. Now was the time to put it in motion.

"One sec!" you yelped, leaping from the bed, shedding the down comforter, and tugging off your clothes.

"Okay!" you signaled. "GO!"

In a mad relay race, I jumped out of the shower and grabbed a towel as you darted, pale and naked, into the space I'd just vacated. Hot water poured over your body as I ducked into the bedroom, steam rising from my skin. "That was flawless!" you called out joyfully, in a voice muffled by the torrential shower. "That was military-style precision!"

I giggled and rooted through your top drawer for a pair of cashmere socks to slip over my feet, which were already returning to their previous arctic temperature. Normally you called me into the bathroom to keep you company while you showered, and while I waited for the summons, I checked my phone (nothing) and e-mail (nothing), wrote $Z + E$ on the windowpane with my fingertip, coiled my wet hair into a bun, and then took it down again. Still not a word came from the bathroom. I perched expectantly at the edge of the bed and twirled my cozy-socked feet for five minutes. Now I was getting lonely. The door to the bathroom was only an inch or two ajar, so I knocked lightly before entering.

"Elise?" I ventured, sliding inside. A jungle mist filled the bathroom, and I could barely make you out behind the fogged shower door. As your figure became visible, a prickle of confusion arose in me. *What were you doing?* I wondered. What *weren't* you doing might have been the more accurate question—instead of exfoliating or shaving your legs or shampooing your hair, you simply stood still beneath the water, head tilted downward and arms at your side. Like a wax dummy.

"Elise?" I tried again, louder.

As if emerging from a standing sleep, you turned to look at me through the door. "Oh hey, Zoe," you said, your words coming in slow motion. I peered closer, trying to distinguish the object that hung slackly in your hand. A toothbrush. I watched in puzzlement as you glanced at the toothbrush, paused a long while, and then returned to brushing your teeth. It seemed that the activity had been interrupted by your trance.

"Is everything okay?" I asked.

"Uh-huh," you mumbled, your mouth still foamy with toothpaste. You spit, rinsed, and placed your toothbrush back on the ledge of the tub. Although the glass blurred your body, I still marveled at how narrow you were in silhouette. Wispier than a stalk of wheat, with limbs like long, fluttering scarves.

I sat down atop the toilet and drew a star on the fogged bathroom sink. "You're so quiet," I said when you failed to start a conversation. The shower taps twisted shut, terminating the sound of rushing water, and I stood to hand you a towel as one wrist emerged from behind the glass. "Thanks," you said softly, taking the offering and wrapping it awkwardly around your body. I watched, bewildered, until I noticed that you were holding something in your other hand. Something fragile.

The door slid open. As you got out, I saw how bony your shoulders had gotten. Spiderlike, almost. Had you gotten too thin? *No*, I thought; it wasn't possible. We'd been eating the exact same thing for months, and if *I* were still far from too thin, there was nothing to worry about in your case. You pulled the towel tighter and avoided my eye. Suddenly I felt like a trespasser—like an unwanted guest. I'd never felt that way before when I kept you company in the bathroom. Why hadn't you invited me in this time?

Your left fist was still closed around something as you opened the medicine cabinet and mechanically pumped moisturizer into your palm.

"What's that?" I asked trying to keep my voice casual.

You kept your gaze trained on the mirror as you rubbed moisturizer onto your cheeks with one hand, despite the fact that the glass was fogged over and no more reflective than a square of concrete.

"Hey," I repeated, tugging at the edge of your towel like a toddler. "What's going on?"

You turned to face me, one hand circling lotion into your forehead. The closed fist extended in my direction. Instinctively I put my hands out, ready for you to bestow whatever you held in your fist like a gift. When you released, however, a web of something wet and tangled fell into my hands.

"What—?" I asked, staring at the matter.

"My hair," you said.

I peered at the bundle in my hand. It was indeed your hair—a pile of white-blond strands massed at the center of an upturned palm. A tumbleweed of hair. I looked up at you in alarm, but your eyes were already scorched with red.

"This was all from—" I started.

"Just now," you nodded. "There's more, too."

A tear wound its way down your cheek, leaving no trace on a face already shining with moisture.

"It comes out in the shower," you said. "I can feel it come out whenever I run my hands through my hair."

I did not know what to say.

"I stopped brushing it last month because every time I was finished, there'd be clots of hair left in the brush."

*Clots.* I reached out and circled my fingers around your wrist, from which a few wet threads still dangled.

"I'm losing my hair," you whispered, the idea breaking over you like an egg cracked against the lip of a bowl. "Zoe, it feels as though my body is preparing to—"

I squeezed your wrist tightly—violently—with my fingers. Your face contorted in pain, but I had no other way of stopping you from saying what you were going to say. And when I let go, your arm dropped lifelessly against your side. A chill winter draft was infiltrating the bathroom, cooling our skin and sucking away steam. I stood to put an arm around your waist, and you slumped against me like a child. Slowly, ever so slowly, I walked you from the bathroom to the bed, where you sat numbly as I wrapped a down comforter around your shivering body. *Pale Elise in a pale blanket,* I thought, holding you close to me. Outside in the darkness, a cotton-white layer of snow was accumulating on the windowsill and atop the trees. You always think the weather will be better by March—a little more pleasant, a little less bitter—but it isn't at all. There is always one last snowstorm. *Perhaps,* I remember thinking abstractly, *tonight will be the night.*

There was no heaving, no sobbing, and no moaning from you: just a steady line of tears following their gravity-bound path. A bruise was already starting to show on your wrist from where I'd clasped you, and I averted my eyes guiltily, staring out the window until I felt the feather-weight mass of your body succumbing to sleep. The front door opened downstairs; your parents had arrived home from dinner. Late, as usual. The bustling adjustments of coat-removal and umbrella-folding drifted up to me, followed by the sharper sound of your mother's heels ascending the stairs. Your bedroom door was closed, so all I had to do was reach over and turn off the light. The sound of clacking heels stopped—in my mind's eye I saw your mother peering down the hallway to check if your light was still on—and then, thank God, the noise commenced once more in the opposite direction. They were probably drunk again. The sound of your father lumbering up the stairs followed and then faded as he entered their bedroom; with this cue I could exhale, safe in the knowledge that we were exempt from parental interference. Not that they would have thought to check in on you, anyway. They paid so little attention to their only daughter.

I carefully unwrapped and got you into bed, trying not to disturb your sleep too much (no cause for worry; you barely stirred). I made sure that the comforter was tucked tightly on your side before maneuvering myself under the covers next to you and crowding in close, shrinking from the frigid air that stung every centimeter of exposed skin. I worried, at first, that our bodies wouldn't be capable of generating enough heat for both of us, but they must have done the job somehow because I soon fell into a deep, dark, and dream-riddled sleep.

When we awoke the next morning, it was still snowing.

Love,
Zoe

# [Day Thirty-one]

*I licked and sealed the envelope,* intending to dash downstairs and drop it off in the box near Alexandra's office before breakfast. It's a quick errand, and one that I perform often, since I tend to write my letters to Elise around bedtime. I headed for the staircase, scraping my teeth against my tongue to remove the bitter taste of envelope glue. My stomach, now acclimated to the Twin Birch diet, rumbled expectantly. What a traitorous organ! I sniffed the air. What was for breakfast? Something with fruit, it smelled like. Behind me, I heard another early riser making her way down the hallway. Probably Jane, who occasionally went to the kitchen early to suck up to Devon by offering to dice fruit and stir the oatmeal pot. There was no point in doing these things—Devon was constitutionally immune to flattery, and therefore impossible to corrupt—but Jane kept at it. Some people are slow to learn.

I kept walking, scanning the high ceilings and delicate crown molding as I went. By now the route was second nature, though the luxury of the house impressed me more with each day. I'd discovered, over the past week, that each item in the house had its own special purpose.

Pieces of furniture that I'd passed without a second thought turned out to have specific functions, like a mahogany table with its own chessboard built right into the top, or a cabinet built to fit snugly beneath the stairs.

Lost in these thoughts, I didn't notice the steps behind me increasing in pace until a few seconds later. *There's no hurry,* I wanted to tell Jane—Devon was never going to give her special treatment for stirring pancake batter. The air was still heavy with breakfast odors as I approached the staircase. What was that smell? Grilled apricots? Waffles with blackberry jam? *Stop drooling,* I commanded myself. *Make your mind blank.*

As I paused at the top of the landing, I registered the sound of footsteps once more. Jane—if it was Jane—should've broken off in the direction of the kitchen. Instead, the footsteps had continued to follow my course toward the staircase. I could think of no reason why anyone but me should require a detour downstairs, and my palm began to sweat around the envelope I held. The footsteps grew closer, nearing the place where I stood. I turned around.

It was Caroline.

She stopped in her tracks a few feet from where I stood, then took a single step forward, her eyes wild with purpose. I blinked. The sun hit my roommate from behind, shining through sparse strands of hair and setting the perimeter of her sweater aglow. She seethed with anger, and I saw that the person who stood before me was no longer the meek and fearful roommate that I'd grown accustomed to. She was, instead, a stranger intent on harming me. *But why—?*

"I know," Caroline said. She took another step forward.

"Caroline," I said, trying to keep my voice low and steady.

"I know exactly what you did," she continued, taking another step. Only an arm's length of hallway separated us.

As her foot slid forward to close the gap, I inched back instinctively, then shrieked: The heel of my shoe dipped over the edge of the staircase and into empty air. I flailed, grasping the banister for support, and pulled myself back up with a noise like a strangled cat.

When I regained my balance, I found myself two steps beneath Caroline, who had been watching my struggle dispassionately from the lip of the staircase. Now she stared down at me from above, and I knew that it was only a matter of seconds before she smacked me or tried to push me down the staircase. *Should I yell?* It didn't matter. By now, everyone was in or near the dining room, settling into her usual seat. No matter how loud I screamed, the corridors dividing us were too mazelike for anyone to discern which direction my screams were coming from. I held my tongue and clasped the banister hard with my left hand as Caroline raised her right arm. I shrank, waiting for the blow, and closed my eyes.

It didn't come.

"You stole Brooke's dress," she spat.

"You're wrong," I said. "Why would I—"

"You wanted to attack her," Caroline said. "Because she knows what kind of person you really are. Someone messed up. Someone we can't trust."

"I haven't done anything!" I sputtered. The envelope in my hand had grown damp with sweat, and now I lifted it to Caroline's eyes. "I'm mailing a letter, Caroline. That's what I'm doing. That's *all* I'm doing." I turned and began taking the steps quickly, my rubbery legs bowing slightly with each pace.

Caroline came after me. "You're a liar," she hissed.

"Follow me everywhere you want," I rebutted, my voice rising. "You already watch me sleep—now you can watch me mail my letters, and eat, and take a shower, and everything else!"

I rounded the bend and headed for Alexandra's office as Caroline stalked behind me. The red box gleamed at the end of the hallway like a beacon. Clutching Elise's letter, I prayed that my sweat wouldn't smudge the address beyond recognition. Upon reaching the box, I deposited my envelope through the slit and turned, furious, to ask Caroline whether she'd gotten her fill. The opportunity never came.

"What are you doing?" she whispered, her glance ricocheting from the mailbox to me and back again.

"What?" I said, regaining my confidence. "There's something about me you don't know?"

"No—" Caroline said, her skin turning ashen. She pointed toward the mailbox. "You said you were mailing a letter."

"And?"

"But you put it in there," Caroline said. She looked bewildered enough to cry.

"I'm not doing anything to anyone," I shouted. "I'm mailing a letter! What part of that is confusing you?"

"That's not a mailbox."

"What are you talking about?" I had no more patience for this. Wiping off my clammy hands, I moved forward, brushing past Caroline in the hallway. Just before I swung a left toward the staircase, she regained her speaking and moving abilities.

"There wasn't even a stamp on that letter!" She shouted after me. "It's not going to get sent."

"For your information, Alexandra stamps them." I continued walking down the hall, faster this time.

"There's something the matter with you, Zoe," said Caroline's voice from behind, and I heard her pursuing me once more.

"Oh?" I called over my shoulder from the foot of the stairs. "I appreciate the diagnosis."

"That's Alexandra's inbox," Caroline blurted, speeding up to match my pace. "It's not a mailbox. We're not even *allowed* to send letters. *You're* the one who can't be trusted! *You're* the one with issues—"

She stopped, clamping her mouth shut as Alexandra strode into the room.

"What's going on?"

A set of keys clanged in Alexandra's hand as she swept toward us from the direction of the front door. She must have overheard the argument when she let herself in.

"Caroline, go to breakfast immediately."

I smirked at Caroline, who looked as though she'd been hit over the head with a bag of hammers.

"*Go*," Alexandra said. "Zoe, my office. Now."

*Good*, I thought. Not only would I get to skip breakfast, but I had a few questions for Alexandra myself—specifically, about whether Caroline had been telling the truth about the letters. Was I *really* the only one allowed to send mail from Twin Birch? Why on earth would I get special treatment?

As I followed the therapist into her all-white office, a section from the Twin Birch memo came back to me with startling clarity.

*Patients arrive over the course of five days, with arrivals staggered so that each patient can receive a customized initiation.*

A customized initiation, I thought, meant that the administrators could control exactly how much information was doled out to each one of us. Naturally, each patient would assume she'd been given the same spiel as the next patient. There'd be no reason to think otherwise.

Alexandra sat down, fuming, but I remained on my feet. A number of queer thoughts were occurring to me at once. For starters, what would it mean if I *was* the only girl allowed to send letters from Twin Birch?

Sensing my inattention to her efforts, Alexandra stood up and zeroed in on where I stood. Before I could protest, she'd taken my elbow and guided me to a sitting position on the couch, and the gesture surprised me so much that I realized what her goal was only *after* she'd accomplished it. With a quick series of movements, she'd manipulated the situation so that she no longer appeared to be my enemy, instead taking on the physical position of an ally.

*No*, I thought. *This woman is not your friend, Zoe.*

"Why am I the only one allowed to send letters?" I asked, not bothering to hide the accusation in my tone.

Alexandra looked at me sympathetically but didn't answer right away.

"You are sending them, aren't you?" I continued. "They're getting to Elise, right?"

"Zoe—"

"Tell me that's a mailbox. Tell me Caroline is wrong!"

"Zoe, please calm down."

A sickening realization dawned on me. "That," I said, pointing a shaking finger at the red box outside the door, "is not a mailbox."

"No, it's not," Alexandra said.

I sprang up from the sofa and began to pace. Alexandra had suddenly become, in my eyes, a person who had unilaterally deceived me for the past five weeks. I didn't trust her, her choreography, or her insipid white leather sofas. I wanted urgently to slash the leather surface to ribbons—to shred the afghans and overturn the chairs. Then I stopped pacing. If possible, the situation was worse than I'd originally suspected.

"Elise hasn't been responding to my letters," I said, my voice spiked with accusation. "I thought it was my fault. But it's not."

Alexandra leveled her gaze at me.

"It's *yours*," I went on. "She hasn't been responding because you haven't been sending them," I said. As soon as the words were out, I knew that I was right.

Alexandra watched me. "It's true," she said. "I have not been sending your letters."

"*That's why she's been ignoring me!*" I yelled. I didn't care if the girls upstairs could hear me. I'd scream loud enough to bring down the house if I wanted.

Alexandra stared back at me serenely, and the sight of her indifference provoked me to further heights of apoplexy. I punched the box of Kleenex on the coffee table, sending it to the ground with a bounce.

"How can you not have sent my letters?" I screamed.

No answer. I slapped the glass surface of the table with every ounce of strength, causing it to rattle menacingly.

"*That's* why she hasn't written me back." Little black stars were scattering across my vision. "Not me. It has nothing to do with me. I hate this place. I hate it!"

"No, Zoe, that's not why," Alexandra soothed, her well-moisturized hands folded over one knee.

"Did you read them?" I pummeled my fists against the couch. "You read my letters. How *dare* you read my letters?"

"I did not read your letters."

This was not happening. It could not be happening. I needed to sit down badly, but I would rather die than touch the wretched sofa again—the sofa where I'd sat, like an idiot, lapping up hours of Alexandra's false empathy.

I melted to the floor, clutching my shoulders. Tears boiled forth. I rocked, trying to force air into my cramped lungs. Then I heard her voice again.

"You know why Elise hasn't responded," Alexandra said from a closer distance this time.

She came to kneel at my side.

"You didn't send them," I sobbed, rocking. "You didn't send them."

"Elise is dead, Zoe."

"*You didn't send my letters.*"

"It's time for you to confront it."

"*You never sent my letters.*"

"Elise is dead."

"*You—*"

"Zoe."

I was going under, I could feel it. There I went.

"*Zoe.*"

I sat very still, like a spoon suspended in Jell-O. Not thinking, just floating.

Alexandra stood above me, her face shimmering through the Jell-O distortion. There was no reason for me to break the surface.

I didn't need to breathe.

# [day thirty-three]

*Elise always said* that there are two types of people in the world: people who lose things and people who break things. She was the kind of person who lost things—subway passes, pots of lip balm, glasses of water, English papers. I am the other kind of person.

Forty-eight hours ago, I finally learned why I'd been sent to this place.

I spent the remainder of that day in bed, watching shadows change shape against the wall. My door remained closed except for visits from Alexandra, who brought food at intervals but didn't make me eat it. All day I hovered in some strange place between consciousness and unconsciousness, though I must have truly fallen asleep at some point because I woke up today to find that it was morning. The light that entered the bedroom had not woken me up. It was too pale and weak, and Devon hadn't woken me up, either. Nobody else was awake, and I figured it had to be around six a.m. Sitting up, I immediately understood what had roused me. The pain originated in a hidden space behind my ear, the left one, and spidered out across my skull, pulsing coolly as it grasped. *No, no,* I said aloud, mainly to register that I wasn't dreaming. There was no roommate to worry about waking with my moans; Caroline had been transferred to Jane's room as soon as our confrontation was brought to Angela's attention. I stood up experimentally. But this worsened the headache, so I got back in bed and waited. The room was silent. There was a knock on the door.

Then it opened. None of the doors at Twin Birch can be locked.

Alexandra knelt down beside the bed and put a hand on my arm.

When I didn't verbally or physically respond, she stood, looked around for a seat, and settled on Caroline's vacant bed. I followed the trajectory of a dust mote as it drifted to the bed-spread in front of me.

"I think it would be a good idea to start talking again," she said. Technically we'd skipped the previous day's session, though Alexandra had been in and out of my room every hour. A session would have been pointless. I could barely breathe, much less talk.

"What time is it?" I asked.

"Eleven thirty, give or take."

Later than I thought. Had I fallen asleep since waking up this morning? The rest of the girls were outside, gardening, hence the absolute quiet of the house. My headache was better, and I hoisted myself up to a sitting position.

"On April 22 of this year," Alexandra began, "you experienced an extraordinarily tragic event."

I found another dust mote to watch.

"Your best friend passed away."

The mote fell.

"Zoe? Stay with me."

Then she repeated what she had already said, and although I'd heard the words before, they still struck me as gibberish. As pure nonsense. It was like bending down to tie your shoes and finding gloves on your feet.

"What you've been experiencing," Alexandra said, "are symptoms of post-traumatic stress disorder, Zoe. Numbness. Detachment. A lack of interest in daily activities."

I wrapped my arms around my chest, pretending that they were stitches holding my body together.

"You've experienced significant memory loss," Alexandra continued. "You've told me many things about your life during our sessions, but your stories abruptly drop off after a certain date. We've talked about nothing that has happened since April 8 of this year."

"April 8?" I echoed. The date had no significance to me.

"The final snowstorm of the season."

"Oh," I said, my voice microscopic.

"According to her parents, that was the last time you saw Elise."

"I can barely survive a week without her," I said, straining to keep my voice from growing agitated. "But two months? Three months? That—"

"Zoe."

Alexandra leaned over and picked a manila envelope up from my bedside table. I hadn't noticed it before—had it been there when she entered?

"You haven't opened it," she observed quietly, gazing down at the packet. *ZOE* was written in plain letters at the top. Returning to her seat on Caroline's bed, she slit open the envelope and pulled out a sheaf of white envelopes, then placed the whole bundle in front of me. I picked up the first and flipped it over. *Elise Pope* was centered neatly on the envelope in my handwriting, followed by her address in Brooklyn. I flipped over the next envelope and saw the same thing. I did not need to see them all to know that they were sealed. Elise hadn't read a word. But still, Alexandra was wrong—her evidence was misleading. Elise hadn't read my letters because Alexandra hadn't sent them, not because she was—

"Hold on," I said. I had a way to prove Alexandra wrong.

I leaned over the bed and felt around underneath for my notebook, which I opened to an earlier page. All I had to do was find my entries from April 8 onward and show them to Alexandra to prove that my memory was intact. How, after all, could I have simply deleted two months of time from my consciousness? Nobody can do that, even if they want to. Amnesia is not a condition that can be attained voluntarily. I paged urgently through the journal as Alexandra waited.

Then I stopped.

There was nothing. I reversed the pages and tried again, going backwards through June.

Nothing.

My entries from winter converged directly with my entries from June, when I had my first day at Twin Birch. Between the two periods, there was no evidence of time elapsing.

"Memory loss can happen," Alexandra said, "after traumatic events. Perhaps it would help if we reconstruct the timeline of what happened. The memories will start to come back to you, Zoe."

I was caught between two versions of reality and unsure of which to believe.

"If we re-create the timeline," Alexandra continued, "you'll be able to see the past more clearly. And you'll be able to come to terms with it."

"Okay," I said softly.

Instead of starting at the beginning, we needed to start at the end.

"Elise died on April 22," Alexandra said.

"Elise died," I echoed, wishing I could erase the words as soon as they were out. How could I tell such a lie? Why was she making me do it?

"Do you remember when she left school?" Alexandra prodded.

I did not remember.

"April 11 was her last day. A Monday. She was hospitalized the following Friday."

I did not believe these things, but without a record in my

journal, I could not prove them wrong. There was no evidence. Nobody believes anything without evidence.

"If this all happened," I said, my voice thread-thin, "how come I don't know?"

"You *do* know. Try to remember."

I squinted, as if trying to bring my thoughts into focus. The memories were elusive and shape-shifting; just when I thought that I'd grabbed hold of one, it ducked my grasp. But something small was coming back to me.

"I remember being alone," I said.

"At school?"

"Yes." The affirmation left a black taste in my mouth, as though I'd bitten into rubber. "It happened so quickly," I said. "She was fine one day, and the next day she was not."

*She was always cold. Even when the snow melted and the spring bulbs flowered, she wore a winter coat. Her hands were yellow from lack of circulation.*

"Her parents took her out of class," I continued.

*There were always hairs on her coat. Her hair was falling out. Strands drifted downward at the slightest movement of her head. Disembodied tangles appeared on her pillow every morning, and sometimes on the collar of her coat.*

"She was so thin," I said. "I couldn't see her anymore."

"Why not?"

I squeezed my eyes shut, casting into the void of my mind for an answer. When it came to me, I bent my head down and mumbled the words into my blanket.

"Can you repeat that, Zoe?"

No, I couldn't. I couldn't speak it out loud.

"You're doing so well," Alexandra intoned.

I lifted my head above the blanket. "I wasn't allowed to see her."

"Why not?"

I knew why.

"It was my fault."

My head dropped forward like a door on a hinge, and I buried my face in the blanket again. It was wet now; I must have been crying.

"It wasn't your fault that Elise died, Zoe. Do you hear me?"

Deeper I went, into the blanket.

"Do you hear me, Zoe?"

A hand on my back forced me back to the surface, where I shook my head *No. No.* I did not hear her. "I was the one who made Elise stop eating," I said. "I made us both do it."

"It's not a matter of blame," Alexandra said. "It's far more complicated than that."

But it wasn't, not really.

"You might have influenced Elise," Alexandra said, "but—"

"No one else did," I interrupted.

"No one else did what?"

"Influenced her."

I looked up. I was starting to see the way things were now, and if I stayed calm and kept breathing, I could explain it all to Alexandra.

"I was the only one who ever influenced her," I said.

Alexandra waited patiently. *She knew*, I realized. She'd known all along exactly what I had done. The whole story was probably typed out in my file from day one.

*That's what Brooke had seen. That's why she was afraid of me.*

Apologies were useless now, and all I could do was confess. This time, I forced myself to look straight at Alexandra as the words exited my mouth.

When we were finished, she left me alone in my room.

# [day thirty-four]

*The crying had a trajectory.* First came bewildered crying, then came angry crying, and, finally, destitute crying. For one more day, I was bedbound, barely stirring except to see Alexandra and to attempt the plain meals that were brought to my room. By last night, I felt as though I'd expelled every ounce of water in my body through crying. I was certain that I was all dried up.

The next morning—today—I woke up and got out of bed. *If I don't get up today,* I thought, *I might never get up at all.* So I slid my feet from beneath the covers, planted them on the floor, and got dressed.

The breakfast room was quieter than it was before, and I was confused to find that both Jane and Caroline were missing from the room. "Where did everyone go?" I asked Devon as I took my seat between Victoria and Haley. Only one of the tables had been set today. A lonely quiet had settled upon the dining room.

"Their session ended two days ago," Devon explained. "Six weeks from the day they started."

I dimly recalled what was written on the memo, though I hadn't returned to it in days. If arrivals at Twin Birch were staggered, it made sense that departures would be staggered, too. I just hadn't realized how little time was left to go.

"You okay?" Victoria asked. I was slumped in my chair, unable to resist gravity. Did she know what I had done? My body was weak from its lack of activity over the past few days. I looked at Victoria, dreading the idea that she knew the truth about me. If she did, how could she be my friend? How could anybody be my friend?

But she just smiled and cocked her head. "Why so sad? We're almost outta this dump."

Of course she didn't know the truth. Why would she?

"Haley's next," Victoria continued. "This afternoon. Lucky girl."

"How do you know?" I asked.

"Easy. We leave in the order that we arrived. You must be last, poor thing."

Of course. I nodded.

"Anyhow," Victoria went on, "you didn't miss much while you were sick."

*Sick*. Had Alexandra provided that excuse for me?

"Not true. You missed one thing," Haley said. "We're allowed to choose whatever we want for our final meal. I asked for carrot cake pancakes."

"Which is, of course, my *least* favorite item on the menu,"

Victoria griped. "The marriage of vegetables and pancakes gives me morning sickness."

I summoned a watery smile as Devon waved us over to the side table. It was odd, being in the dining room without the other girls—who, I wondered, was first to leave?

Since there were only the three of us, we didn't have to take turns. I'd eaten very little over the past couple of days, and for once I welcomed the sweet, mellow pancakes without anticipating how awful they'd make me feel. As it turned out, they didn't make me feel bad at all. Just full.

I sleepwalked through the rest of the day, catatonically helping Victoria and Haley prepare for their afternoon pickups. We emptied drawers and folded button-ups and jeans that no longer fit into nylon suitcases. Neither of them asked what was wrong with me—instead, they politely chalked it up to my "sickness" of the previous few days and didn't get frustrated when I spaced out for minutes at a time. We collected and tossed out bottles of depleted shampoo and conditioner, leaving the bathroom counters depressingly bare. Victoria's flight to New Orleans was going to leave in the early evening, and Haley was due to be picked up any minute for the long trip back to Arizona. When Haley's parents' silver Lexus charged up the driveway at three o'clock sharp, we hugged goodbye and promised to visit each other. I should have cried—Victoria did—but there was nothing left in me to come out.

After Haley's departure, the house was as quiet as a tomb, and Victoria and I decided to spend the rest of the evening outside on the grass. Classes were suspended, but Devon checked in on us every hour to make sure that we were unharmed. The two of us lay still, staring up at the trees, not talking much but not sleeping either. Victoria must have sensed that something was up, and she wisely gave me the space to think about it. We sprawled quietly within inches of each other, combing our thoughts in solitude with the reassurance that we weren't entirely alone. I zoned in and out of the present. Mostly out.

The spell was interrupted when Victoria's ride to the airport arrived. We sat up, brushing wisps of grass from our pants. Victoria's face was already crumpling at the prospect of saying goodbye, but I stopped her.

"You're fine," I said. "You're doing so well."

*And you're better off without me.*

"We'll talk a lot?" she asked, her eyelashes matting together with wetness. "Every day?"

"Whenever you want," I lied.

Victoria nodded, and then she did something surprising. She hugged me. At first, I didn't know what to do and stood there stiffly, my arms at my sides. But then I did something that surprised me, too. I hugged her back.

We walked silently inside to fetch her suitcases. Angela spoke with the driver for a few moments, double-checking that he knew the correct airport and terminal at which to deposit his passenger. Victoria climbed in and waved bravely from the backseat, pressing her other hand against the glass. The face framed by the window looked different than it had a few weeks earlier. The puffiness was gone, and though Victoria still looked precarious—like a glass vase so breakable it makes you nervous just looking at it— she also looked beautiful. Sweeter, somehow, and more innocent.

I waved back as the car picked up speed, smiling as I said a different sort of goodbye.

### Carrot Cake Pancakes for Long Goodbyes

1 cup whole wheat flour

1 cup all-purpose flour

2 ½ tsp. baking powder

2 tsp. cinnamon

½ tsp. nutmeg

½ tsp. ginger

¼ cup raisins (optional)

1 tbsp. orange or lemon zest

3 tbsp. maple syrup

1 tsp. vanilla extract

2 eggs, lightly beaten

1 cup almond milk (or soy milk, rice milk, regular milk)

½ cup grated carrot

Mix dry ingredients and raisins together. In another bowl, mix wet ingredients, excluding carrots. Make a well in the center of the dry ingredients and pour wet ingredients in. Stir, but don't mix too much. A few lumps are fine. Fold in the grated carrots. If batter is too thick, add more milk. Cook pancakes as usual, then serve with walnuts and maple syrup. (These can be made using any pancake mix, too. Just add spices and raisins to the mix and prepare according to instructions, folding in carrots at the end.)

Eat pancakes with loved ones to celebrate

friendships—bittersweet when they end, and hopeful when they are only just beginning.

I turned and walked back inside, wondering when my mother was scheduled to pick me up.

And then there was one.

# [day thirty-six]

*My suitcases were packed;* I had nothing left to do. I walked downstairs. I had one more question to ask Alexandra.

I found her in her office, working over some notes. "I have something to ask you," I said from the doorway.

"Come in," she said. "What about?"

I sat down on the sofa, unsure of how to phrase my query, and doubtful, besides, about whether Alexandra would even know the answer.

"The photos on Caroline's dresser," I said. "The ones that she arranged in a row—"

Alexandra nodded, signifying that she knew what I was talking about.

"I've been wondering the whole time who that was."

Alexandra put down her pen. "You didn't ask Caroline?"

"She wouldn't tell me," I said. "Was it her brother? Her nephew?"

"Neither," Alexandra said.

"Then—?"

"The pictures were of Caroline."

The next question was obvious, so I asked it. "Why?"

"Caroline would be able to tell you better herself," Alexandra said, slowing to plot her words carefully. "My sense is that the photographs reminded her of a time when her life was uncomplicated. When she was small and happy, with nothing to weigh her down."

I nodded.

"Why do you ask?" Alexandra asked.

"Just curious."

That was all I wanted, so I said goodbye to Alexandra and went to bring my suitcase down from the bedroom. A car churned gravel in the distance, drawing closer to the building. My mother. I thought about Caroline's photos as I dragged my things down the hallway. In the end, what she'd wanted was to bring her old self back to life. I understood.

Travel does funny things with time. It starts as soon as you step on the plane or in the car, and it doesn't stop there. When you're away from home, time stretches and bunches like taffy: A week can feel as long as a month or as short as a day. You never know. You can't predict it. That's why I keep a journal when I travel— not so that I can preserve my memories for the future, but so that

I can stay oriented in the present. Otherwise, forget it. I'm lost on arrival.

I consider coming to Twin Birch a kind of travel. It's not a remote destination by geographic standards, and I didn't have to get on a plane to come here. But in other ways, it's a faraway land. The currency is different and the accommodations foreign. Neither of those things matter much, though, when you dig down to the core of it. No. The beautiful thing about travel is that it promises change. Real change. You can go on vacation and come back a new person. Maybe you change; maybe you just look at things a different way.

In a way, that's what happened at Twin Birch. I am not the same Zoe that I was six weeks ago.

By the time my mother came to pick me up, my bedroom was empty. Clothes were folded and packed away. While she took care of arrangements with Angela downstairs, I lifted one of the sole remaining personal objects from beneath the bed and held it in my hands. In the lilac evening light, it shone an unearthly shade of white. My name was printed on the front of the manila envelope in big block letters. *ZOE.*

I reopened it, running a finger beneath my name. Then I pulled out the stack of smaller envelopes contained within. The handwriting was recognizable but askew—like a photograph that somebody had Photoshopped just slightly. The envelopes were neither stamped nor postmarked. None had been read.

My suitcase was downstairs, zipped, and waiting by the door. Soon enough I'd hear the familiar sound of car wheels churning over gravel—although this time, I'd hear it from the passenger's perspective.

I reached beneath the bed and pulled out the box, removing its lid to survey the supplies within. Unsurprisingly, they were diminished from their original abundance. The container had initially been heavy with paper goods: practically a portable stationery store. Now, there were only a few envelopes, a sheaf of note cards, two stray pens. *How many words had I put down?* I wondered. Add it all up and you'd have a record of our friendship. Elise and me.

A story about two girls.

She would never disappear, I realized. And neither would I.

is there such a thing as fate? A story
about love, destiny, and what happens
when you stop and listen to the music.

JORDANNA
FRAIBERG

OUR SONG

FIRECRACKER